Kalindi

{Brahmankanya}

~ A NOVEL ~

Shridhar V. Ketkar

Translated from the Marathi by

Shanta Gokhale

SPEAKING TIGER

SPEAKING TIGER BOOKS LLP
125A, Ground Floor, Shahpur Jat, near Asiad Village,
New Delhi 110049

Originally published in Marathi in 1930
This translation published by Speaking Tiger Books in 2022

ISBN: 978-93-5447-389-0
eISBN: 978-93-5447-390-6

10 9 8 7 6 5 4 3 2 1

Typeset in EB Garamond by SÜRYA, New Delhi
Printed at Shree Maitrey Printech Pvt. Ltd., Noida

Contents

Translator's Note vii

1. Leaving Home 1
2. Manjula 6
3. Two Generations 11
4. Appasaheb's Family Life 15
5. Manjula Looks at the Future 21
6. The Morality of the Times 26
7. The Siblings Meet 30
8. After the First Flush of Love 39
9. From Despair to Hope 49
10. A Heart-to-heart Chat 57
11. A Woman Has a Question 69
12. Kalindi Leaves Pune 85
13. Shivsharanappa 93
14. First Days in Mumbai 100
15. Esther Keeps Her Promise 103
16. Appasaheb Dagge 107
17. Ramrao 112
18. Friendship Blossoms 118

19. Kalindi Visits Pune 124
20. Satyavrat's Letter 129
21. Kalindi's Advice to Ramrao 135
22. Appasaheb Looks Back 141
23. Vaijanath Shastri: The First Dose 145
24. Kalindi's Decision 156
25. Ramrao's Ideas 159
26. Mill-owners Are Upset 165
27. Aaba Meets Esther 169
28. Ramrao Decides 175
29. The Friends Make a Plan 180
30. A Young Man Pursues Usha 183
31. Confession 190
32. A New Sentiment Awakens 198
33. Shivsharanappa Returns 204
34. A Letter of Revelations 213
35. Changing the World 218
36. The Happy End 225

Translator's Note

Each new novel that one translates makes its own unique demands, as much on one's ability to understand it as a piece of literary invention as on one's skill in transporting its words and world, sense and sensibility through an alien language into an alien culture. Answering every such set of specific challenges involves walking the tight rope between fidelity to the original and fluidity of the resultant text. It is a tough but ultimately rewarding task—one that I must say, translating *Brahmankanya* has been.

To understand *Brahmankanya* as a piece of literary invention was no problem. I had read it often enough before I decided to translate it. I knew it well, warts and all. Belonging to the literary culture that had produced it and fully aware of the circumstances under which it was written, I could easily overlook the flaws. However, as a translator, I could not expect my readers to be similarly understanding and forgiving. In order to help them see why the flaws I refer to existed in the first place and appreciate the manner in which I chose to address them, I must briefly introduce the author, his life and his working style.

Dr Shridhar Vyankatesh Ketkar was a man driven by

deep sociological concerns and convictions. Born on 2 February 1884 in Raipur, located in the Central Provinces under British rule and in Chhattisgarh today, he had to move to his uncle's home in Amravati following his father's premature death. After school, he joined Wilson College in Bombay but left for America before graduation. He did his graduation, Masters and PhD from Cornell University, his special interest being sociology. His PhD thesis was titled, *The History of Caste in India*. *Brahmankanya* reflects that preoccupation.

On his way back to India, Dr Ketkar spent a year-and-a-half in England where he met and fell in love with Edith Cohen, a German Jew. He continued to correspond with her even after his return in 1912. Back home, he soon began to dream of publishing an encyclopaedia in Marathi comprising selected writings of Indian and European scholars that, through juxtaposition, would demonstrate how traditional and advanced systems of knowledge could temper one another to create a new India. He worked at the idea tirelessly till he found two other scholars willing to come on board. Together they registered the project as a limited company with headquarters in Nagpur and a branch in Pune.

The project required a translator who could work from German. Edith Cohen was a fine translator. The company offered her a job, which she accepted with alacrity. She arrived in Pune where Dr Ketkar had moved, in December 1919. Being very much in love, the couple longed to marry. However, perhaps because the system of civil marriage was not available then, a way had to be found within the Vedic system to enable them to do so. Poring over the shastras, Dr Ketkar discovered an ancient rite called vratyastom vidhi whereby a brahmin could legitimately marry a vratya, a 'vile' outsider not born a brahmin. A way had been discovered but no priest in Pune was willing to conduct the ritual. Ultimately Ketkar's associates, Yeshwant Date and Chintaman Karve, stepped in and Edith Cohen became Sheelavati Ketkar. Dr Ketkar and Sheelavatibai made the oddest couple when they walked through the streets of Pune, hand in hand, to buy groceries and vegetables. They were mocked and harassed by conservatives, but their love and convictions ran too deep for fleabites to affect them.

Dynamos that they were, between 1920 and 1930 they managed to publish all twenty-three volumes of the encyclopaedia. During this time, Dr Ketkar also published several scholarly papers, founded and ran three magazines and wrote five novels, each with a strong sociological theme. *Brahmankanya*, published in 1930 and widely regarded as his finest, was the fifth.

The encyclopaedia had drained Dr Ketkar's resources. His last years were spent in dire penury. He, his wife and two adopted children often had to go hungry. One day, a nail pierced the worn-out sole of Dr Ketkar's shoe. He was diabetic. The wound would not heal. He did not receive the quality of medical attention he required in the crowded public hospital where he was admitted and died within ten days. Sheelavatibai, who outlived him by some forty years, has written a restrained but profoundly moving account of their life together—*Meech he Sangitla Pahije* (I alone can speak of this).

Dr Ketkar's novels were derided by several though not all contemporary writers and critics. The popular novelists of the time wrote in the manner of second-rate Victorian writers whose names we have now forgotten. Their novels abounded in simpering damsels and upright young men with whom they fell in love. The prose style was florid, the locations, situations and dialogue unreal and the endings invariably happy. The novels were so anodyne that they would not have rocked a drifting plank, let alone an entire boat. Dr Ketkar's novels, on the other hand, were aimed at rocking boats. He was a man with a mission, impatient of the inequities he saw around him and bent on correcting them. Not surprisingly, many called his novels didactic. Indeed, two leading writers of the time declared they were not novels at all. His language, they said, was shoddy, his characterization flawed and his themes inappropriate. Dr Ketkar's response was, 'You have fed for too long on imitations of conventional English novels. My way is my own and better than yours.'

Reading *Brahmankanya* today, one sees that Dr Ketkar's critics were partly right; but so was he. In his first three novels, his craft was indeed deeply flawed. His plots were rather haphazardly structured, his prose was careless and his dialogue tended to heaviness. In comparison, his later work showed a better command over craft, perhaps because the reduced pressure of work on the encyclopaedia allowed him more time to concentrate on his fiction. Whatever the reason, Dr Ketkar's prose in *Brahmankanya* is crisp, the characters perfectly fleshed out, the dialogue fluid and the narrative structure controlled except for three instances where he allowed himself to get carried away.

There is a forty-page chunk in the first half of the novel which contains what purports to be a 'true' story appearing in a popular magazine of the time. It is written in the form of letters between a young woman and the man she loves who later betrays her, leaving a question mark over her life. While the story has some bearing on important events in *Brahmankanya*, and incidentally provides amusing proof of Dr Ketkar's sharp eye for the overblown prose women wrote in popular magazines, its inordinate length holds up the narrative at a time when the future of the chief protagonist is hanging in the balance.

Again, towards the end of the novel, nearly twenty pages are devoted to a fictional scholar's incomplete Smruti or code of law that proposes a new social order based on matriarchy. This digression too, straying from the narrative for too long, tries our patience. In the third instance, the author is caught up in explaining the involved details of a scheme that an important character, a textile mills union leader, has conceived for the betterment of workers.

When I re-read *Brahmankanya*, this time as a translator rather than as an admiring reader, I saw clearly that my task lay beyond translation. I would have to edit the text as I went along. I have therefore condensed the three passages mentioned above, dropping the lengthy letter form of the first, the sutra form of the second and the confusing details of the third. What we have here is, in effect, a retelling of the original. Besides these major departures, I have also tightened passages where the author has repeated himself.

These problems would certainly have been set right in the original had Dr Ketkar had the services of a good editor. As it happens, there was no time for editing. His novels were serialized in magazines before they appeared as books. The author once rued this manner of working. 'I write under pressure from the compositor,' he said.

Once I had decided to edit *Brahmankanya*, translating it was smooth sailing. Dr Ketkar writes an economic prose that lends itself very well to English. His sensibility, too, is modern which again facilitates translation into English. Finally, located in urban centres like Pune and Mumbai, the novel has very few culture-specific references that the translator needs to get around. All in all, translating *Brahmankanya* has been a joyous and creatively fulfilling journey.

Shanta Gokhale
Mumbai, 2022

1. Leaving Home

Intrepid champions of women's education in the town were deeply grieved to hear Kalindi's story. What can one say about Kalindi's parents? They were filled with such disgust at her reckless behaviour that they swore never to see her face again. The townspeople were thrilled to have a spicy titbit to chew over. It is time we provided a full account of what Kalindi did to bring such shame on her family.

Kalindi was studying in the final year for her Bachelor of Arts degree. Her parents fully expected that, when she passed, she would be widely felicitated; that the news would appear in the press and her photograph in illustrated magazines. But now all their expectations were dashed. Kalindi had dropped out of college. That was not all. She had left her parents' home to live with a merchant named Shivsharanappa as his mistress. Shivsharanappa, a Lingayat by caste, owned a tobacco shop in Bhavani Peth. His car had served to ferry voters when Kalindi's father had stood for the municipal elections. Kalindi's parents were naturally furious with Shivsharanappa. But what use was that? They could not even drag him to court for seducing their daughter. She was twenty-one years old after all. We have minted a coin that has turned out false they said to themselves, swallowing their anger in silence.

Kalindi's father, Appasaheb Dagge, would even have married Kalindi to Shivsharanappa to provide a moral cover for an immoral act. But how could he do that? Shivsharanappa was already married. Moreover, his mind was not calm enough to allow him to think rationally about how this wrong could be made legally right. Appasaheb was angry with his daughter not so much because she had done herself harm, but because she had brought him infamy. However, given his family history of the last couple of generations, he could not be certain that any efforts on his part could have assured her of a better future than the one she had chosen for herself. We must recount that history to understand why Kalindi did what she did.

When Appasaheb Dagge married, his moral courage was praised sky-high and his liberal spirit greatly applauded. Needless to say, the praise came chiefly from self-serving people. Appasaheb was young at the time and Kalindi's mother Shanta was known to be a well-educated and beautiful girl. Well-educated did not mean university educated. She had passed the fourth or fifth grade at school. In those days, this meant well-educated when referring to girls. There were people who even declared vehemently that if Hindu society wished to think of itself as civilized, it could not refuse to accept a well-educated girl like Shanta just because her mother's life was blemished. However, a suggestion had been made earlier to the mother by those very people whose hearts bled for social reform.

They suggested that she should 'put sentiment aside, look at the issue practically', persuade the girl to convert to Christianity and marry a Christian youth.

It was common for beautiful, well-educated girls to become the subject of discussion in college canteens and even lawyers' chambers. Appasaheb Dagge, who had recently been awarded a bachelor of law degree, had had an argument with a colleague about Shanta. 'Why should the girl convert to Christianity?' he had demanded. 'Are there no men of courage in our Hindu community who will marry her?' This question had travelled all over town and reached the ears of Shanta's mother and the man she called her husband. A few days later the 'husband', Dr Chintopant, requested a meeting with Appasaheb. He praised Appasaheb for his liberal spirit and reformist views and, by the end of the meeting, had persuaded him to marry Shanta. Dr Chintopant then went about town praising Appasaheb for taking the reformist cause forward. While Dr Chintopant and some of his friends applauded Appasaheb's progressive views, others declared him 'an ass who has corrupted his caste by falling in love with a girl for her beauty'. Others went further. They wondered if there was not, perhaps, some grave flaw in Appasaheb himself, unknown to them. He must surely have some ulterior motive in agreeing to marry the girl. Some senior lawyers surmised that this could be Appasaheb's ruse to gain favour with 'Mahadeo Govinda' (the term they snidely used for the reformist Justice Mahadev Govind Ranade), in order to ensure an early promotion to the post of Munsif for himself. Needless to say, nobody knew with any certitude Appasaheb's actual feelings in the matter.

This is how he had put it to himself: 'Brahmins are a liberal people. Those who are thrown out of the caste today will surely be taken back tomorrow while those who are in today and consider a daughter to be a blot on the family, will be out tomorrow. The brahmin caste will be thrown open to all. Once that happens, the age when a Matsyagandha, a fisherman's daughter, gave birth to a sage will return and brahmins will be responsible for uniting all castes.' It is on the strength of this argument that Appasaheb married Shanta.

Then Dr Chintopant died. He had not made a will; so his entire estate went to his legitimate son alone. Serves Appasaheb right people said gleefully. But Appasaheb had not married Shanta for Dr Chintopant's money. He would not have touched any part of it even if she had got a share. In his opinion, that would have quite corrupted the altruistic motive for which he had married her—which was to make brahminhood all-inclusive.

Appasaheb wished his wife would forget her past. Having married a brahmin, she had to assert to herself that she was a brahmin woman. Shantabai never had the courage to do that. The pressure of her background lay so heavily upon her that, if she made the least pretense to social prestige, she was sure people would sneer at her. Her great regret at what Kalindi had done stemmed not from anxiety for her daughter's future, but from her own feeling of inferiority. Now people would say, 'Like mother like daughter. After all the soil is the same.' She shrank at the dirt that was going to be thrown at her because of her past.

Kalindi knew she had lost the good opinion of people. She knew her family and friends must be cursing her. Her act had so repelled people that newspapers, generally most eager to publish scandal, had gone silent over it. Kalindi had no wish to visit her family, nor for them to visit her. Her wish was granted. Not only did her family not visit her, even her friends stayed away, although some at least would have liked to know why she, a well-educated girl, had decided to live with a man out of wedlock. They had discussed this back and forth. The only way to understand her point of view would have been to talk to her. But their families would never have tolerated that; and they lacked the courage to defy them.

If we are to understand the reasons that led to Kalindi's act and the cause of her parents' anger against her, we must go back to a story that relates to her grandmother, Manjula.

2. Manjula

There must be very few people in Pune today who still remember Manjula, the schoolteacher. Although it has not been long since she died, she had not been in the public eye for almost a generation before that. Indeed, even those who remember her, do so because of the scandal attached to her name.

Not many people had seen Manjula grow from childhood to youth. The few who had, declared that she had been unquestionably beautiful as a young girl. However, even they did not know what caste she had belonged to. Some thought she might have been from the washer-man caste. Others thought it could be the cowherd, oil-presser or bangle-seller caste. The only thing everybody was agreed upon was that she was not a brahmin. And yet, nobody dared say she was not, because everything about her declared her to be so—her looks, her habits, her language. In fact many believed she must be from some minor sub-caste of brahmins at the least.

The truth is: Manjula was not a brahmin. She had studied up to the fifth or sixth grade during the early years of women's education and become a schoolteacher. It was then that her life had taken a turn and become the subject of general gossip. During those early years of women's education when it was impossible to find upper-caste women to work as teachers, the education department employed women from lower castes who had managed to get an education. Manjula was one of these women.

Manjula had been married at the very young age of four or five. She had continued to live with her parents as was the custom, and enjoyed going to school. She was always neat and tidy. With the cultural values she acquired at school, she felt a deep desire to refine herself in such a way that she would be mistaken for an upper-caste girl. With this in mind she set about consciously emulating the brahmin lifestyle.

Manjula became a teacher when she was about sixteen. Her husband, who lived in some remote place like Talegaon or Junnar, had been trying very hard, from the time she had achieved puberty at thirteen, to bring her home. This too was the custom but she had refused to go. Nor had her mother insisted that she must. Later, when she became a teacher, she began to feel ashamed of her illiterate husband. Not only was he a country bumpkin, but he belonged to one of the lower castes. With the efforts she had put into acquiring upper-caste habits, she found the idea of living with him demeaning and repugnant. The husband on his part was not about to give up his conjugal rights. And so she consulted a lawyer to find out if she could get out of the situation with the help of the law.

The lawyer initially advised her to deny that she was married at all. She could claim that the ceremony she had been through was engagement, not marriage. It helped that she had continued to use her maiden name at school. The lawyer proposed to use this as evidence to support her claim. In those days it had become customary for young married girls or child widows to use their maiden names if they were going to school, because they were embarrassed to have people know the truth about them. This custom is still followed in Pune. However, there would have been many hurdles to supporting Manjula's claim that she was not married. Most importantly, it would have been difficult to prove that her wedding ceremony was actually an engagement ceremony. The lawyer decided he would have to devise another strategy.

In Manjula's caste a woman could, by custom, discard one husband to marry another. Taking advantage of this, the lawyer advised Manjula to demand maintenance of Rs 500 from her husband for the three or four years that she had stayed in her parents' home after puberty, and to send him a legal notice to say that, if the sum was not paid within a week, she would marry again. Manjula did accordingly through the same lawyer. As expected, her husband could not pay the amount she demanded; and so he was forced to give up his rights over her. Manjula had set herself free. Too free as it turned out. Her life now took an unexpected turn.

Manjula had always cherished a wish to be part of educated society. She was young and beautiful. So people were very happy to have her come home to tutor their sons and daughters. As it turned out, tutoring was only a cover for carrying on illicit relationships. There were many of these in the years that followed. But it was her relationship with Dr Chintopant that lasted till the end. Her conduct after she entered into this relationship was blameless. She was true to him all his life. Her children were his children. This relationship had been so unquestionably accepted by society and by his first family that Dr Chintopant's children often visited her; and if the father scolded them occasionally, she rushed to defend them.

One of the children Manjula bore Dr Chintopant was Shanta, Kalindi's mother. Manjula worried about Shanta's marriage. But meanwhile, she did a wise thing. She educated Shanta to whatever level she could so that, in the event that a husband could not be found for her, she would be equipped to earn her living. As we have seen, she did not need to support herself. Way beyond Manjula's expectations, a young brahmin lawyer, Appasaheb Dagge, married Shanta. In those days, the custom was for men like him to marry young pre-pubescent girls. Appasaheb considered this wrong. He also believed the caste system to be wrong and knew that the only way to break it was through inter-caste marriages. Moreover, he was looking for an educated wife. Shanta fitted his expectations perfectly. And she was beautiful to boot.

In those days even ordinary men demanded dowries. Here was Appasaheb, a young man with a law degree. He could have demanded and got a truly handsome dowry. But when a man with liberal ideas marries, nobody dares talk of money. No money changed hands when Appasaheb's marriage was solemnized. Dr Chintopant praised him duly for his ideas, but began to believe, privately, that he was a foolish young man. He had agreed to marry a girl with a blot on her past and still not asked for a dowry. Newspapers carried brief reports of the marriage. They too applauded Appasaheb for his laudable act, not failing to mention pointedly that the girl was actually from a 'good' family. It is not surprising that Shanta did not appreciate this extravagant praise for Appasaheb which underlined the great good turn he had done her.

3. Two Generations

Manjula was relieved of her worry about her daughter's marriage. Armchair reformers told the world how wonderful it was that a social problem had been solved. As it turned out, however, the problem had not been solved. It had merely been passed on to the next generation. Shanta gave birth to a daughter. They called her Kalindi. She had siblings too; but it was Kalindi about whom Shantabai began to worry as she was growing up.

Kalindi was now eighteen years old. Her parents were not as worried about her marriage as their neighbours were. Appasaheb was confident that, just as he had married the daughter of a kept woman, some worthy young man would step forward to marry his daughter for her good looks and other virtues. He waited for a letter from some such young man that would declare his passionate love for his daughter and ask for her hand. He even imagined the words in which the letter would be couched. The youth would declare that his daughter was a goddess and that he himself was entirely unworthy of her. Appasaheb would then consent to his suit with much satisfaction.

However, the event that he imagined never came

to pass. Rather, it did not happen in the way he had imagined. A letter did come but one that angered him immensely. The man who wrote it was not from the caste he had desired or expected. Educated and bright though he was, he was the son of a dancing girl. Indignant at his request for Kalindi's hand, Appasaheb said to himself, 'My daughter has been born in wedlock. Does this man think this virtuous and beautiful girl belongs to his class? I did not marry Shanta to push my family down into a dancing girl's caste. I married her to prove that even a dancing girl had the right to enter a higher caste. It was to light a new hope in the lives of the downtrodden. Not to push myself and my descendants down into that class.'

Appasaheb showed the letter to Shantabai and Kalindi, making a brief speech about the young man's arrogance in considering himself equal to Appasaheb while ignoring the noble purpose that had prompted him to marry Shantabai. Shantabai did not say a word after his speech. She could not deny her husband's generosity in marrying her. But Kalindi could not resist saying, 'Who can say today whether you married Aai out of a liberal impulse or a desire for fame? As it happens, your children's status does not come from the nobility of your intentions. Your generosity did no harm to you but it has greatly harmed your children's future. In what way did you suffer for your liberalism? Only to the extent that priests would not officiate at your ancestors' death rituals. But you remained a brahmin, your status intact. And what are we?' Kalindi's question was direct.

Kalindi's younger siblings laughed to hear her ask it.

Appasaheb noticed and was taken aback. He saw now that his children did not regard his generosity towards their mother very highly. Instead, they appeared to think their father had entered into an improper marriage for fame and they, rather than he, were now suffering the consequences. Appasaheb Dagge had never imagined that his own children would blame him for an act which, in his view, had been unquestionably honourable.

Appasaheb was more than a little upset to see his children laugh. 'So do you want to marry him?'

Kalindi replied, 'I haven't given any thought to marriage yet.'

Taking this as her answer to the young man's application, Appasaheb instantly wrote off to him turning down his request. As she grew older, Kalindi's thoughts about the affair took the following shape: The offer for marriage had come walking to their door unbidden. Appasaheb had disapproved of it. He had given her no information that would help her decide, but rushed her for an answer. Thus he had, in fact, deceived her. From then on, she saw her father as one with whom she had grave differences and began to suspect his good sense and indeed the purity of his intentions.

There was one person, however, who stood up on Appasaheb's behalf in this situation. That was his son Satyavrat, Aaba. He said to Kalindi, 'You are thinking of yourself only as Baba's daughter when you blame him for not having married a brahmin girl. But think of yourself as Aai's daughter and then ask yourself if he did right in marrying her or not.' Satyavrat's argument pleased everybody except Kalindi. 'That thought doesn't satisfy me either. I simply don't want this unstable social status of being neither here nor there.' His daughter's dismissal of his courageous act was not the first time that Appasaheb's family had blamed him. They had blamed him often enough before this.

4. Appasaheb's Family Life

In the early months of marriage, Appasaheb Dagge was happy in his life with Shantabai. For some time he continued to glow with pride at the thought of his courageous act. There were people who still praised him for it. But their admiration faded away in a year or two. Appasaheb loved nothing more than to hear praise of his moral courage. Outwardly, however, he would pretend he had done nothing out of the ordinary in going against tradition in his marriage. He would assert quite firmly that if people thought he had been cheated, they were wrong. That was not all. He continued to believe what he had said to a friend before his marriage: his wife was a woman of virtue and untouched by the tainted nature of her mother's life. He defended his act by quoting a Sanskrit verse which meant: 'Take nectar even if it tastes like poison; take gold even if it lies in shit; take knowledge even if it comes from a low-born wretch; take a virtuous woman even if she comes from a disreputable family.' He even tried, with complete sincerity, to imbibe the attitude that the couplet counselled.

However, it was not at all easy to follow it. Although

he thought of his wife as virtuous, that opinion did not extend to her mother. Consequently, he felt strongly that his wife should not visit her mother. He could never rid his mind of the suspicion that his mother-in-law's ideas about morality were bound to be somewhat loose. Therefore, although mother and daughter lived in the same town, barring the first few months after marriage, there was no coming and going between the two houses.

For a while Shantabai thought her husband was right in objecting to her visiting her mother. She too was keen to show that she had nothing to do with her mother. However, that changed over time. Shantabai began to think that her husband's prohibiting her from visiting her mother most certainly demonstrated his lack of faith in her. Although this was how she felt, she did not make her thoughts known. She told herself that she and her husband had a loving relationship. Why then should she start a quarrel over wanting to visit her mother? For some time she resolved to see her mother only when she visited her but would not herself visit her mother. Later she had to tell her mother that her husband did not approve of her visiting either. With that, there was an end to all communication between mother and daughter almost till the day the mother died.

Appasaheb was very optimistic about his family's future. He was convinced that his caste would be passed on to his progeny. It was important that he should not allow his brahmin culture to slide and that his wife and children should emulate it. This made it vital that they not visit Shantabai's mother. Despite Manjulabai having assimilated brahmin ways and language and assiduously followed them, Appasaheb had observed that traces of the time she had spent in a lower-caste environment did sometimes show through. He feared that his family might unconsciously emulate her and those ways would enter his home. His desire was that his wife should erase every sign of her past and imbibe fully the new ways of thinking and behaving that she was now exposed to.

Appasaheb, on his part, kept company only with those brahmins who were liberal in their religious outlook. However, the same could not be said for Shantabai. She sensed no problem when she sat among other women in the Prarthana Samaj hall; but the normal give and take of social life forced her to face many bitter truths. Several men visited Appasaheb in his home. They even had tea with him. But their wives did not visit Shantabai. Some women would say she must visit them first and they would be happy to return the visit. However, on the several occasions that she did, she noticed her hostess would take care to dress in a plain six-yard sari and not the formal nine-yards for fear of it being polluted. And although she would herself serve Shantabai tea, once Shantabai had touched the cup and saucer, the maid would be called in to take them away. Not that these experiences were new to Shantabai. Before marriage, she had noticed that when she visited her brahmin friends, she would be treated differently from the brahmin girls who were visiting with her. But in those days she rarely visited these friends. After her marriage, however, she was compelled to keep company only with brahmins. When her husband told her that she must make efforts to erase her past, she could not but say, 'However much you may want to erase my earlier life, the world will not let you.' When she described to him how women from reformist homes treated her, Appasaheb would say, 'How can you expect brahmin women to treat you as an equal merely because you are married to a brahmin? They will naturally treat you as they would have had you married in your caste and class.'

Shantabai would then say, 'If brahmins treat us in this discriminating manner, why should we insist on mixing with them?' To this he would reply, 'My dear, we should mix with brahmins not in our interest but in the interest of the brahmin community. We want to make them more liberal in their ideas. How will this happen if we stay aloof from them?' Husband and wife saw the problem from different points of view. The wife wanted to be happy here and now. She did not want any part of the brahmin community and their contemptuous 'liberal' treatment of her. Making brahmins more liberal was not her mission. She would rather live with people who did not consider her touch polluting. Whom to socialize with remained a perennial bone of contention between Appasaheb and Shantabai.

The fact that Appasaheb had married outside his caste did not mean he had lost his caste pride. When Shantabai complained about the brahmin women's behaviour towards her, Appasaheb did occasionally feel she was criticizing 'his' caste. It was 'his' caste he had hoped to make more liberal when he had married Shantabai. 'The social future of Hindustan,' he would say, 'is dependent on the social morality or policy of the brahmin caste. It is only within the brahmin community that we find genuine opposition to caste discrimination. A brahmin who stands against it is inspired purely by a noble social ideal. When members of other castes protest against it, they do so entirely out of envy. When caste discrimination is abolished, it would have to be by brahmins. If we grant that the caste system can only be destroyed through inter-caste marriage, we must also concede that this can only happen when brahmins open their ranks to other castes. For theirs is the only caste into which members of every other caste would be happy to marry. If this is not happening yet, it is because they fear the consequences of their action. Once more and more brahmins marry out of their caste, the fear of consequences will vanish simply because there will no longer be consequences. That is why it is important for brahmins to become liberal. Once that happens the country will be united. When he spoke of these convictions at home, Shantabai would laugh in a way that showed disbelief.

There were other points of conflict between them too. Whenever reformists and newspapermen praised Appasaheb for his liberalism, Shantabai would take it as an affront to herself, while they remained totally unaware that they were causing offence. She looked forward to the day when this hurtful practice that showed her up as an object of charity would end. Although she did not openly talk about her feelings, Appasaheb sensed them and so he spoke to a couple of his friends about it and brought the constant harping on his noble act to an end. When Shantabai heard about this from him sometime later, she felt deeply grateful to him for putting greater value on her hurt than on his own pleasure in being praised.

Their marriage presented no problems beyond these minor conflicts while they were by themselves—husband and wife. But when a daughter was born to them, they felt they had created a new life with an uncertain future. They wondered if it was a good idea to continue living in Pune where everybody knew their family history. Perhaps it would be better for their children if they moved to a different town. However, the idea did not get translated into action and they remained in Pune.

Shantabai was happy when Satyavrat was born. 'When the boy grows up, he, being a man, will have the strength to fight against all problems.' But meanwhile, the children would soon start going to school, would be made to feel different, would be teased. Once again the idea of moving away surfaced and once again it was followed by inaction. This time they felt certain that their family history would follow them wherever they went. Their marriage had made headlines when it took place and Dr Chintopant was known all over Maharashtra. So the Dagges continued to live in Appasaheb's home town, Pune.

5. Manjula Looks at the Future

Dr Chintopant died a few years after Appasaheb and Shanta married; but Manjula outlived him by twelve years. Appasaheb had permitted Shantabai to visit Manjulabai during her last illness. Shantabai's half-brothers were also present that day. When she died, the gold ornaments that had come to her from Dr Chintopant were sold and, in accordance with her will, the proceeds distributed equally among the siblings. Appasaheb was furious. Although he had not cared for money in his youth, he had begun to care for it after his children came. His professional earnings did not amount to much. Surely Manjulabai knew that his children were precariously placed, that they had no real blood relations, that getting them married would be difficult on his meagre income? How then could she have made such an ill-conceived will? Had she not made a will at all, her entire property would have come to her daughter. Brooding over the noble reasons for which he had married her daughter, he wondered bitterly how she could not have remembered the great favour he had done her.

Shantabai on her part, although saddened by her

mother's death, was disappointed that her expectations, built on things she had heard, had been dashed. It was said that a mother's estate goes to her daughters. Here she was, the only daughter. Should she not have inherited all that her mother owned? It must be noted that her estimate of what her mother owned was way off the mark. She had thought her mother's property was worth at least twenty-five thousand rupees, perhaps even fifty. But when her ornaments were sold, it turned out that the amount was a mere three thousand. This made Shantabai richer by a mere one thousand rupees. The house in which Manjulabai had lived, Gavtya Gomajicha Wada, also turned out not to be in her name. Although Dr Chintopant had promised to make it over to her in the early days of their relationship, he had kept putting it off. By the time Manjulabai realized he had gone back on his word, it was too late to do anything about it. She had lost her youth and with it the hold she had had over him. She thought if she nagged him then about the house, she might lose even what she had. She decided it would serve her better to be patient and hope Dr Chintopant would do something of his own accord out of pity for the mother or love for the child. The other reason why she decided to leave the matter of the house alone was that her daughter did not care enough for her even to visit her. Why risk losing everything by nagging Dr Chintopant for the sake of this daughter and son-in-law who looked upon her with contempt? After all it was Dr Chintopant's sons who cared for her. They possibly did this because being kind to their father's second wife would bring them praise. But the fact remained that they cared and her own daughter and son-in-law did not. Manjulabai had left behind a letter addressed to her daughter. This is what it said:

Dear Shanta,

Since your marriage, our circumstances have turned out to be very different. You are the wife of a respectable man and I the mistress of another. That is the big difference between our situations and the reason why you have kept away from me. I do not blame you, nor do I accuse you of ingratitude. I am sure what is driving you is concern for your children's future.

A mother's heart always belongs to her daughter, however much she might hurt and insult her. A mother understands precisely why her daughter behaves the way she does. In fact, I would myself have advised you to do what you are doing. All I want is for you to be happy.

Be that as it may, I must admit I see a dark future for your children. I do not think your marrying a respectable man was a thing to celebrate. Dr Chintopant should have married you to someone with a similar history as yours. You would not have held aloof from me then, nor would your husband have expected you to. By allowing you to marry into respectability, I have pushed you and your children into a state of constant fear and uncertainty. I now believe we deceived your husband into marrying you by flattering him—a young man—for his progressive ideals and giving him false notions about the praise he would win with a deed such as this. Praise or no praise, we cannot remain blind to the fact that far from turning a bastard child into a respectable woman, the respectable man she marries will himself face becoming an outcast. This will lead to who knows how many generations of remorse and, most certainly, to regret for both husband and wife in the present.

You must face the fact that you will never be accepted in your husband's caste, nor indeed even among lower castes like the Shenvis, Sonars or Prabhus. If you dream of marrying your children into any of these catses, you will have to do it deceitfully as we did. And thus, the cycle of deceit will continue from one generation to the next. Perhaps your husband feels the strain of the situation already. He might not blame you for it. However, the less he blames you the more he will blame himself, leading to a level of mental stress that he will find difficult to endure.

And yet, when a young man placed similarly as Kalindi asked for her hand, your husband was offended by the proposal and turned it down. It saddened me to hear about it. I think pride is preventing you from seeing the future that is in store for you. But your mind will never be easy until you accept that your husband's community will never accept you.

People sing paeans to truth. I never did believe in its worth, particularly where a mother is concerned. A mother's religion is love of her children. There was a time when I considered it a mother's duty to hide her daughter's defects in order to place her in a beneficial marriage. This was not only my view, but the general view. However, I did the opposite when the time came. I hid nothing about you when I asked your husband to consider our proposal. Perhaps it was not such a virtuous thing to do. Dr Chintopant was a well-known man. Your background was known not only in the city, but all over Maharashtra. Had this not been so, I would not have thought twice about hiding your background to get you married to a brahmin if I had thought it was in your best interests.

Be that as it may, I have now come to realize that truth is the only way. I would advise you not to hide the facts of your birth when you are looking for a match for your daughter. Hiding them will never assure your children's entry into the brahmin caste. The right 'castes' for your children are widowers, bastards and such others. I would advise you to encourage your children to seek their life partners among them.

This is what I have been wanting to say to you.

With my blessings,

Your mother Manjula

Needless to say, this letter acquires significance in view of the path Kalindi chose for herself.

6. The Morality of the Times

Kalindi's act had an impact on her younger sister Usha's life. She discovered that after Kalindi left home, young men began to look upon her as a woman of loose morals. They would call out to her whenever she passed by and make propositions or lewd gestures. Usha was furious with Kalindi for causing her this daily humiliation. Gradually, however, the young men who loafed around the streets of Pune lost interest in her. Soon her anger against her sister also mellowed.

Satyavrat, on the other hand, was not angry at all, only deeply intrigued. He wanted to know what could have driven his sister to take the entirely unexpected and incomprehensible step—one that stood against all moral principles of their society—of leaving home to live with a man as his mistress. As it happened, he was away from home when she left. Believing in acquiring a wider experience of life by changing place and company, he had convinced his father to let him join a college in Mumbai for one term and then travel around the country. Kalindi had left home during his absence. He wondered whether the discussion they had had before these events about his friend Shinde's second marriage, should have warned him about her views on the institution of marriage.

Although Shinde was a few years older than Satyavrat, they played cricket together, which made them good friends. Shinde was a Maratha by caste and had been married while still a boy. He did well at college, won a scholarship, went abroad and returned as a barrister. He then declared his intention of getting married a second time. He soon received a proposal from a family of repute for their young, educated daughter. Kalindi happened to know the girl and was certain she was unhappy about the proposed marriage. But it turned out she was wrong. When Kalindi asked her, 'How do you feel about marrying a man who has a wife already', the girl said, 'But that wife isn't educated. She will never have a hold over him. I am educated and younger than her. My hold on him will be forever.'

This girl was thinking only of herself. The idea that her marriage to the barrister would perhaps be an act of injustice towards the first wife did not even enter her mind. Nobody asked Barrister Shinde why he was marrying a second time when his first wife was alive. Kalindi wanted to know and got her brother to ask him on her behalf. Shinde said, 'The idea that one shouldn't marry a second time while the first wife is alive is British. I am expected to accept this restriction because I have had a British education. The British marry when they are old enough to earn their living and they choose whom to marry. I did not have that choice. The British can divorce a first wife and marry again. In emulation of brahmins, good Maratha families believe it is wrong to divorce their wives. If I don't have the freedom of choice that British men have, and unlike them I cannot divorce my first wife, why should I accept the restrictions that are imposed on them? If I were to repeat what was once the custom among upper-class Marathas, I would say the higher a man's social status, the more wives he must have.'

When Satyavrat reported Shinde's answer to Kalindi, she said, 'So what do you think of it?'

'Tell me what you think of it,' Satyavrat countered.

'I think there's truth in what he says. And you?'

'I think only one thing. Shinde will argue his cases well.'

'Why do you say that? What's wrong with what he says?'

'If even you think he is right, then his falseness turns into truth.'

'Why is he false according to you?'

'Every individual in India is married as a child. But they don't all take a second wife when they grow up. Shouldn't Shinde live by the rules that educated people in our society have accepted? How can he set himself up as different from the others? Why are you taken in by his argument?'

'Perhaps I am not so concerned about whether he should or should not marry. I am more concerned that the girl has agreed to become his second wife. Perhaps she is lured by the fact that he's a barrister. But I still feel you should think further about what Shinde says. His basic argument is, should we accept the restrictions that the British have adopted when we don't have the freedoms they have.'

'Perhaps the principle behind his argument is right. But does everyone who has been married as a child have the freedom to marry a second time?'

'If you agree that the principle is right, then to behave in accordance with it is also right. If he draws censure for his act, I would go further and say he has acted with courage. If more people like Shinde refuse to suppress their natural instincts for fear of what people will say, it might even lead to the end of child marriages.'

Satyavrat could not think of a convincing response to Kalindi's argument. But he remained dissatisfied with it. Meanwhile he decided that Kalindi's opinion on this case was a sure sign that she was becoming rebellious. However, he continued to mull over the problem, wondering whether denying one's desires was indeed a way of closing the door on the possibility of social change. When Satyavrat heard about Kalindi's decision to leave home, he told his parents about this conversation, suggesting that it might be considered as a hint of the direction in which her ideas were moving. He did say, however, that he was not prepared to condemn her action outright. He saw it as a consequence of the social and moral instability of their times.

7. The Siblings Meet

Shivsharanappa had been a client of two generations of Appasaheb's family—his father's and now his. That had made him a regular visitor to their house. Appasaheb was an old-style Hindu father. Kalindi could not talk to young men who were single. But he had no objections whatsoever to her talking to young men who were married. He had even fewer objections if the man was Muslim. Kalindi was therefore allowed to talk to Shivsharanappa and, since there were no rules that went beyond talking, there was nothing to prevent a friendship from forming between the two.

It became a habit for Shantabai, Usha and Kalindi to go for a spin in Shivsharanappa's car. If he happened to be around when Kalindi was leaving for college, he was even allowed to ferry her there. Shivsharanappa had money but little education. It was easy for Appasaheb to regard him as a servant. He could never have imagined that Kalindi would think of him as an equal. Appasaheb was not free of the usual aspirations of parents wanting to marry their educated daughters to young men in the civil service. Needless to say, impecunious young men were ruled out of the race. He was not out to ruin his daughter's life. It must be admitted here that his position on social issues had been shifting over the years. Did he insist on a brahmin son-in-law or would one who was merely rich do? Would he have been as upset as he had been if the man who had written for Kalindi's hand in marriage had been educated in England and was drawing a fat salary in government service? We cannot be sure; but perhaps he might then have concluded that an inter-caste marriage was the only way to quicken the pace of social change. However, if his prospective son-in-law was not a civil servant or a barrister, then he had to be brahmin.

Satyavrat on his part wondered what could have brought about this impossible intimacy between Kalindi and Shivsharanappa and why he had not suspected what was going on. Unfortunately, parents and children had little communication in the Dagge home. Appasaheb had never openly discussed his children's future with them. He relied on one thing alone for Kalindi's future—his certainty that there existed young men who would look at her education and ignore her family history as he had done with Shantabai. So all he needed to do was give her maximum education to make her value in the marriage market unassailable. He did not realize that the value of educated girls had depreciated since his days because the supply of high-caste educated women had soared.

Although there was no communication between father and children about their future, the brother and sister talked constantly with each other about their circumstances. This had assured Satyavrat that Kalindi would trust him enough to confide in him if occasion arose. That she had not told him about Shivsharanappa suggested that she did not trust him.

This was indeed true. Something that had happened before Satyavrat left to join his college in Mumbai had damaged her trust in him. The event that had led to a heated argument between the two was a Pune girl, Saraswat by caste, daughter of a widow who had remarried, marrying a Muslim man. Satyavrat said it would have been better for the girl to remain single than to marry a Muslim. He argued that there could be no objection to a Hindu man marrying a Muslim girl because that meant the Hindu community was winning another member. Kalindi's opinion was very different. But she saw that her brother was fundamentally opposed to women having the freedom to choose whom to marry. It was hardly surprising for her to conclude then that whatever decision she took with regard to her future, would have to be done without confiding in him.

It was about a month after she left home that Kalindi began to go out and about. Once she had gone to see a play at Lakshmi cinema house. It so happened that Satyavrat was sitting in the row behind her. She saw him when she turned around. The expression in his eyes indicated two things—that he was upset with her and that he would like to speak with her. After a while she excused herself to Shivsharanappa saying she wanted to go out for a while. On her way, she signalled to Satyavrat to join her. Once outside, Kalindi got into her car, asked Satyavrat to step in and told the driver to drive to Sunkersett Road.

The driver got a little suspicious. He was new. He

had never seen Satyavrat before. He asked if they were to wait for the boss. Then he took out a foot rule and pretended to measure the petrol to see if there was enough. He was obviously stalling for time when he noticed Shivsharanappa emerge from the theatre. He came up to the car and instructed the driver to take the lady to some place where she could take in fresh air and bring her back in half-an-hour. Turning to Kalindi he urged, 'Do come back in half-an-hour. The play is worth seeing after that.' The car which the driver had previously found difficult to start suddenly leapt forward now and was soon speeding towards Swar Gate. When it turned into Khadakwasla Road, Kalindi asked the driver to pick up a pack of cigarettes for Satyavrat and have a cup of tea himself. The driver understood what this meant and left.

A silence ensued. Neither sibling was quite sure who should begin to speak and what they should say. Finally Kalindi said, 'How are Aai and Baba?'

'They're well,' Satyavrat replied.

'I suppose everybody at home hates me.'

'I wouldn't say hate. But they are saddened by your thoughtless action.'

'I don't care what else they hold me responsible for, but surely not thoughtlessness. You know I am not thoughtless. I have tossed and turned in bed without sleep for days thinking. You are aware of that. I may be immoral. But not thoughtless. How can you of all people think that of me?'

'Tai, I used the word thoughtless because my tongue was incapable of pronouncing the word immoral. But that in fact was the word in my mind. And yet it is difficult to use it about you, who are so honest in everything you do. You are always forgiving of other people's shortcomings but you use a stern eye for your own. That is why I have always had the highest respect for you. And that is why I thought your action had to be the result either of strong emotion or a fit of madness.'

'Do you really think I'm mad?'

'Well, I can never think you are capable of an immoral action. I say it was a fit of madness because I can't think of any other reason that could have driven you to it.'

'If you can't think of any other reason than that, I will say you are unbelievably forgetful. That makes you weak in mind or perhaps even mad.'

'How am I forgetful?'

'You are forgetting the arguments we have had.'

'Oh? Which arguments?'

'Remember the discussion we had when Manjula Aji wrote that letter?'

'But then you were of the opinion that we should try our best to find our place in the brahmin community.'

'I did indeed think so then. But I don't think so now.'

'Why is that?'

'I don't think a community that has always held us up to scorn is one that I want to spend my life trying to break into and in the process look for a generous-hearted brahmin to marry and in the bargain be guilty of the immorality of ruining his life in order to serve my interests.'

'And so?'

'And so, the only thing one can do is enter a caste

that is even more scorned than us. It has been a well-established rule of our society that those who reject caste discrimination are destined to marry bastards or widowers or other such social outcasts. We are all aware of the rule. That is why we don't dare marry outside our caste. It has become fashionable to speak against caste discrimination because you earn praise for it these days. But the only people who truly reject caste discrimination and are willing to include all comers in their community are the bastard caste. Since Bramho beliefs have gained influence in our society, a few cattle have strayed from the flock, but they are so few that they haven't been able to form a herd of their own and have had to fall back on other outcasts for support. Every word that Manjula Aji wrote in her letter is absolutely true.'

'So this is the future you see for reformers who wish to break the shackles of caste?'

'I don't even accept the existence of those so-called reformers. If they exist, then yes, this is the future I see for them.'

'That would be a very sad thing.'

'Why sad?'

'Because I don't want such a future for myself.'

'Whether you do or don't, it is the only one that awaits you. If you think you will find a girl to marry who is not the daughter of a bastard or a prostitute or at most a destitute brahmin widow who has no other choice, then you are living in a fool's paradise.'

'You are saying these things out of rage against the bitter experience you've had in our family. But surely you don't really believe that people who genuinely want to break the caste system don't exist?'

'Oh, I grant the existence of people who are noble enough or principled enough to say the caste system should be abolished. But none exist who will actually do anything about it. Those who speak theoretically about the issue, do so because they have no idea what lies in store for them in the practical world if they act on their ideas. Ask them if they will turn their principles into action if they know what lies ahead.'

'If such a picture of the future were to be made public, would the movement for abolishing the caste system not lose strength?'

'Where is this strength in the first place for it to be lost? Upper castes are fully aware of what happens to the progeny of mixed-caste couples. Even reformers must know it although they will not admit to it. Or perhaps they choose to be blind to the truth.'

'So according to you, the supporters of the movement must publicly announce they belong to the bastard caste in order to prove their genuineness.'

'Yes. That's about it. Ask them to make the pronouncement and see them suddenly fall silent. Because while they are making all their noble pronouncements, they have nothing but scorn for those who have been cast out by society for no fault of theirs. We don't want such charlatans among us. I'd say abolish them first.'

'Alright, Tai. I accept your argument. I also accept that it was wrong of our father to have scornfully rejected the man who asked to marry you because he belonged to the bastard caste. But now let me ask you about your action. You are living with a man who is not your husband. Why did you not marry a deserving bastard? Because of what you—an educated woman—have done, people are saying you have brought women's education into ignominy.'

'I don't care what people are saying because I know exactly why they are saying it. They are afraid that my action will promote the idea that educated women run off with married men, reducing their educated daughters' value in the marriage market. They couldn't care less about women's education itself. If they truly valued an educated woman, they'd have accepted a woman like me into their family rather than holding what happened in my family two generations ago against her. Why should I care about their daughters' future when they have shown no care for mine?'

'Tai, are you really as embittered about the world as you sound?'

'There was a time when I was embittered. There is not a shred of bitterness left in me now. In fact, I now look at the world and my future with the greatest joy.'

'Joy? What could be your reason for joy?'

'It is the joy of having broken the chains of an imposed situation. I am happy that I have given up forever the desire to force myself into a caste that is supposedly respectable.'

'But don't you give any importance to legal marriage?'

'Why should I?'

'Why shouldn't you? Do you see no value or profit in legal marriage?'

'People marry for two reasons. One is to ensure their

children have a rightful claim to their property. The other is to ensure that they do not become social outcasts. If you don't care about money and property and if, because of a mixed-caste marriage your children are going to be social outcasts anyway, what do I gain by going through a legal marriage blessed by religious rituals? If I marry with the blessings of religion, I will begin to hope that religion will save my children from being outcasts. If that isn't going to happen, harbouring false hopes will only destroy me. If my children are not to be accepted in society, then my wish to marry will be construed as a desire to ensure my material future. Which in turn means that I will have sold myself in order to establish my right to food and shelter. I don't mind being called thoughtless or immoral. I don't want to be taken for a woman who has used love to ensure her material well-being.'

Satyavrat could think of nothing to say in response to Kalindi's argument. So he veered instead onto another track. He said, 'Kalindi, have you forgotten what we used to say? That the institution of marriage might have its failings but it is not wholly without its strengths. So there is no reason to reject it wholesale. We also said that reformers who were trying to create a new society by breaking the caste system were not attacking the institution of marriage.'

Kalindi merely smiled in response. Before Satyavrat could say anything further, the driver returned with his pack of cigarettes and they could not continue their discussion. The car turned back and sped towards the cinema house.

8. After the First Flush of Love

A year after Kalindi had that long conversation with Satyavrat, she gave birth to a boy. They called him Chintamani. Kalindi's mother felt a great urge to see her grandchild. She slipped out of the house without informing her husband and went to Kalindi's house. We cannot positively assert that the mother was fully convinced that her daughter had done no wrong. What we can say, however, is that she felt some sympathy towards her. When she saw how well she was being looked after although she was not Shivsharanappa's wife by marriage, she found herself saying, 'Men look after their mistresses better than they do their wives. The wife is a worthless being, tied to the husband and unable to escape. It is not so with the mistress.' She went further and said, 'Women allow themselves to be needlessly overwhelmed by ideas of morality and respectability and end up mourning through life with their so-called social prestige intact.' Looking at it practically, she did not think her daughter had served herself too badly although morally she had perhaps done wrong. After all, a European nurse had delivered Kalindi's baby, she had a car at her disposal and her wardrobe was full of the latest designs in blouses and footwear. The daughter's luxurious life appeared to dazzle the mother.

Kalindi merely smiled mildly at her mother's observations. She did not let her see what lay in her heart. Although she made a show of happiness, she was inwardly disturbed. Her feelings and ideas had undergone a change after she had left her home. The first couple of months had passed happily. She and Shivsharanappa were pleased with themselves for the manner in which they had defied old ideas of morality. They sniggered at people who belonged to that way of thinking and found their action incomprehensible. They pitied their narrow understanding of human life and the smallness of their minds. But once they had said all that could be said about such people, they were left looking for other things to talk about and there were none.

Shivsharan began to tire of his educated mistress. That he should tire of her was natural. Although he was rich, his ideas about life were not. He was, after all, a grocer by profession and caste. He was keeping her in style only to prove that he knew how an educated woman was to be treated. But, as days passed, he cared less and less about impressing her or anybody else. In the neighbourhoods where he conducted his business, fellow merchants had been used to hailing him as 'the barrister's son-in-law', which tickled his ego no end. But soon that too stopped. After his son was born, the tide turned in the opposite direction. He found that the goodwill he had earned in his business was slipping away. His concentration too was being affected by his relationship with Kalindi. This began to cause him losses. He realized that he was spending much more on her than he had ever spent on his mother, wife and himself. He began to resent her. He thought he had bought himself an expensive toy which he could ill afford. He submitted to the notion that she had lured him into a trap. Resentment grew into bitterness when he realized that he could not tell Kalindi what he could and did tell his wife, that the year had been bad for business and they needed to be thriftier.

Kalindi on the other hand wondered why Shivsharan never shared anything about his business with her. He seemed to think of her only as a good-time companion, not one to whom he could open his heart and mind. She was right. Shivsharan was convinced that, having given her the impression that he would always keep her in comfort, he could not now reveal the other side to her. He certainly did not think of her as his partner in joy *and* grief. She was meant only for joy. The distance that had been growing between them on account of how they viewed each other, intensified after the birth of their son. Shivsharan had already spent something like three thousand rupees on her in a year. Her delivery had cost him four hundred more. Not only had that money vanished into thin air, but with it had gone the interest he would have earned on it.

Kalindi had already begun to review her earlier opinions about the life she had chosen for herself. She had mistakenly taken Shivsharan to be not just a grocer but an educated man, interested in things other than his trade. But she soon discovered it was not so. He did not measure up to her intellectually. That caused her attitude towards him to become tinged with disdain. As she lost respect for Shivsharan, she began to wonder if she was not continuing to live with him merely for his money. Suddenly she saw herself as a mistress rather than a self-respecting woman. This is not how she had expected to feel when she chose to live with a man outside marriage.

When her son was born, she began to examine another one of her earlier notions. She had once dismissed marriage as unnecessary for her children to have legal claims of any kind, because whatever she did, they were going to be treated as bastards. But now she wondered if her reasoning had been right. A conflict arose about this in her mind. Was she that thoughtless woman who had ruined her child's future by having him out of wedlock? She re-examined yet another idea she had once cherished. The love of a woman who lives with a man without demanding marriage is purer than that of a woman who marries a man in search of security. Now she wondered whether any man at all was worth the kind of love that made a woman give up all thoughts of security and the future of her children.

The sense of insecurity that overcame her caused another emotion to take hold of her. Jealousy of Shivsharan's wife. She could not very well say to him: stay here, do not go to her. But she had begun to say she missed him dreadfully when he did not come to see her. She also decided that a woman in her position had to use wiles to hold on to her man. A wife could afford to be neglectful, but not a mistress. Shivsharan in his simple way thought he should relieve her of the loneliness that was the natural outcome of her living outside of all social intercourse. So he bought dozens of books for her, a gramophone and vinyl of popular songs. She thought he had brought her those records because he enjoyed the songs himself. But when she played them during his visits, she suspected they bored him. Then she heard from a servant woman that when his wife Thayamma sang Kannada songs, he listened to her with great pleasure.

She realized Thayamma was in a position where her husband could never throw her out of the house. The institution of marriage had been created to keep a woman secure. Kalindi's youth and beauty were not enough to ensure it. She needed the support of religion and the law to allow her her rights. If she had rejected the institution of marriage for love then surely it was not right for her to continue with a man whom she no longer respected, let alone loved? This was the point she had arrived at in her examination of herself and her situation when her mother made those observations during her visit to her daughter. It was this internal churning that had caused her to smile weakly in response to them. Needless to say, Shantabai had failed to catch the shade of bitterness that lay behind the smile.

Kalindi's unhappiness at the thought that she was perhaps not living with Shivsharan for love any longer, but for material benefit, was intensified further by the thought that she was depriving another woman, Thayamma, of her right to those benefits. She was also destroying that woman's happiness by stealing what belonged to her. Undoubtedly the birth of her son had brought some joy into her life; but again the joy was not unmixed. She imagined the boy growing up and regarding her with resentment for having acted not in his best interests as a mother should, but against them. It was natural that she should ask herself the next logical question. With everything pointing to the fact that her high moral stand about the institution of marriage being only for those who sought security and material benefits, not for those who came together for love, had been proved hollow, she first wondered whether any two human beings could ever be so well-matched that the woman should find it worth burning all her bridges as she had done for a lifetime with the man. Her answer was, perhaps not. The next question was, if she had begun to doubt whether she could sustain the life she had chosen, should she not leave Shivsharan? If she should, the next question was, could she? Shivsharan could ask her to go if he so decided. All he would lose was the money he would have to contribute for their son's maintenance. He would not have to pay anything for hers because he would owe her nothing. But if she left him, she pictured what her life would be like. First, there would be no going back to her parents. That door was closed. In the outside world her status would be of an unmarried mother. Even if she had education, what value would that carry in the face of the social censure she would suffer? What right would she have to complain either?

Shivsharan was not in any better state of mind than her. His business was suffering. There had always been some people in his community who disapproved of him for what he had done. His fellow traders stopped cooperating with him. There were those who condemned him for squandering money on luxuries. In view of this, they felt it was best to be extra cautious about transactions with him. There was another consideration that led to their disapproval. Not only had he kept a mistress, it was rumoured that he even ate the food she cooked. His community had no objection to men keeping mistresses. Why, even a Muslim mistress would not have caused them to raise their eyebrows. What did, was eating her food. These things disturbed his community enough for them to ask him to present himself before the Committee of Elders. Shivsharan refused to face the Committee knowing full well that he would be told to mend his ways. Since he remained absent from the meeting, a decision was taken unilaterally. The community was advised to break all business relations with him.

Thereafter, Shivsharan's fortunes plummeted. He could no longer afford to keep Kalindi in the large flat where he had made a home with her. Renting out the flat, he took her to Shukravar Peth, a distinctly poorer neighbourhood, and rented a single room there for her to live in. He also took away all the ornaments he had given her when they started living together. Finally, he sold off his car as well. As time passed, he was unable to give her the monthly sum of twenty-five rupees that he had promised her. Gradually, his visits to her became rarer. When he did come, he would talk to her curtly. He even took to suggesting that she would do well to join a theatre or cinema company where they were looking for educated women from good homes. When his monthly payments became irregular, she was forced to go to his shop for the money. When he saw her coming, he would move to the backroom and tell his assistant to say he had gone out.

When she saw no escape from the situation in which she was thrown, Kalindi, far from leaving him, decided to do the opposite. If he was in a bad way, she told herself, it would be a sign of her love not to complain about it, but to support him by making do with whatever she got. Shivsharan took this as a sign of abject helplessness, which left her with no option but to make do without complaint. After some time, he stopped visiting her altogether. It was evident to everybody that their relationship was on the point of collapse. Taking advantage of this, all kinds of men took to visiting her to lure her into their arms. Getting wind of this, Shivsharan reviled her as a loose woman. 'You are cheating on me,' he thundered.

Kalindi saw this as the end. There were only two choices before her. Either she killed herself or decided to take control of her life and make a future for herself. Although she knew this is what she must do, it was not easy to act on it immediately. She sought an interim refuge. Who was it who really cared for her? It should have been her parents. But she knew how determined they were to keep up appearances. Satyavrat was the only ray of hope. She wrote a postcard to him saying: 'We have not met for more than a year. Please come to see me when you have the time.' Her address was at the top of the postcard so he would know where she now lived. But Satyavrat neither came nor did he acknowledge her letter. She was bitterly disappointed. Even then, she decided to take another chance and wrote him a proper letter in which she said she had decided to live independently and could she count on his support?

For a long time, a poem from Goldsmith's *Vicar of Wakefield* had been playing on her mind.

When a lovely woman stoops to folly
And finds too late that men betray,
What charm can soothe her melancholy?
What art can wash her guilt away?
The only art her guilt to cover,
To hide her shame from every eye,
To give repentance to her lover
And to wring his bosom is to die.

In such a situation, what could Kalindi expect even her brother to do? Why then ask for his support and pull him down with her? And so Kalindi tore up the letter she had written. She did not know that her postcard lay at home unread by the addressee because he was away from home. Appasaheb wondered if there was any point in forwarding it to him. What he himself gathered from the card was that Kalindi had moved to Shukravar Peth. Seeing the address at the top of the postcard, he and Shantabai realized that her fortunes had fallen even lower. Appasaheb remarked to his wife, 'The wretch will end up in the gutter one day.' He could not think of how he could help to better her condition. And so he neither said nor did anything, pretending that his silence was the result of his justified anger against her. Shantabai's heart was torn for her daughter; but what could she do about it either? Even she did not believe asking Kalindi to return home would be the right thing to do.

Kalindi's ideas about the world had come from poetry. It was only when she was pushed to Shukravar Peth did she see the world as it really was. One way and another, she had lost her family. Her parents' love clearly had its limits. Her father did not want to have anything to do with a daughter who had caused him loss of face in society. Her mother felt that, all said and done, however wrong her behaviour, she was their daughter. But she cared too much for her ideas of status to visit her daughter in a neighbourhood like Shukravar Peth. Satyavrat should surely have come to see her. She wondered why he had not. Lack of time was definitely not enough reason to explain this. Finally, the truth of it was that her family had abandoned her in her time of need.

She knew she could no longer continue to live off Shivsharan now that he found it so difficult to support her. She would have liked to help him in his work but he was not prepared to let her do that. She knew what the moral thing to do under the circumstances was. She had to leave Shivsharan. And go where? One day when she had least expected it, a helping hand was extended to her, temporarily solving her problem. The story of how it happened follows.

9. From Despair to Hope

Kalindi had come to a decision to leave Shivsharan and make a new life for herself. But many days passed and she suffered a series of internal upheavals before she could act on her decision. One day a trivial incident was responsible for setting off a chain of thoughts. The room where Shivsharan had lodged her abounded in insects and lizards. She would often watch lizards waiting for an insect to come within reach and making a grab for it. She saw this as a symbol of how the world worked. It was a cruel world in which human beings preyed on and fed off one another. But on one particular night, an insect that sensed a lizard eyeing it in motionless silence, leapt off the wall as soon as the lizard made a move and fell on a dark spot on the ground where it could see nothing. The thought came to Kalindi then: 'If a tiny creature like this insect can take a leap in the dark to survive, why can I not have the courage to do the same?' She made up her mind to leave the house the very next day without asking herself where she was going. That would be decided once she had made the first move.

The next morning she packed some of her essential

belongings into a large tin trunk, took her son by the hand, hired a coolie to carry her luggage and directed him to the bus stand from where buses left for Mumbai. She got into a waiting bus without bothering to find out where it was headed. When the conductor came to give her a ticket and asked where she wanted to go, she had no answer. He said, 'Do you want to go all the way?' She said 'Yes.' The bus moved. Half an hour later, it stopped at the Khadakwasla lake. She got off there. Sitting beside the lake she wondered why she should not hire a boat, row out to the middle of the lake, tie a stone around her neck and leap in with her son. But before doing that, she wanted to record the reasons why she had decided to take her life. This was not to justify herself but to show how Shivsharanappa was just as guilty of doing wrong as she was and indeed society itself for holding some people in such contempt that they were left with no chance in life and no alternative but to destroy themselves. She began writing the document in the form of a letter to her brother Satyavrat.

It was four o'clock in the afternoon by the time she finished writing the letter. People had begun to gather around the lake gradually for an evening of fresh air. She noticed a group of nurses from Sassoon Hospital and several Europeans who had driven down in their private cars. Some Bene Israels had also come. One of the women noticed her and called out, 'Kalindi'. Turning around, Kalindi recognized her old school friend Esther Killekar. She snapped her notepad shut. Suddenly she felt suffused with a feeling of warmth. Here was a friend from old times, someone with whom she had shared a lovely friendship although she was a couple of years senior to Kalindi at Hujur Paga, their school. She recalled the times when they had got up to all kinds of games and mischief. She remembered how they had concocted a rumour about a secret love affair between two of their teachers. Later, at college, they had fought to have women admitted to the gymkhana committee which did not permit them to stand for elections. Many more such memories engulfed her; but she repressed them and merely smiled at her friend.

Esther began to bombard her with questions. 'What are you doing here? Who is this child? Is he your son? You didn't even tell me you were married. When did that happen?' Kalindi was so used to the whole world knowing her story that she was genuinely surprised to discover that Esther had not heard a word of it. It was natural that she had not, because she belonged to a community that kept to itself and was not a recipient of news from other parts of Pune. Kalindi answered Esther's questions with a quiet, 'I will tell you everything later, if I can stay with you for a few days. Can I?' Esther was shocked at the request. 'Why? What's the matter?'

'I don't have a home,' Kalindi replied.

'Have you fallen out with your family? Have you left home?'

Once again Kalindi said, 'I will explain it later. But may I?'

Esther stared at Kalindi for a while. She realized there must be something terribly wrong for her friend to make such a request. Finally she said, 'Of course you can come.

I am not rich like your father. But if you don't mind a small house, I'd be happy to welcome you there.'

Kalindi arrived at Esther's place incognito. She had erased the vermillion mark on her forehead and assumed the name of Mrs Appa. While some of Esther's neighbours took her to be a Hindu widow, others thought she was a Bene Israel. Consequently, for the first time in years, Kalindi felt free to move around and be herself. Shukravar Peth was never to see her again.

In the next two or three days, Esther had heard the whole story. She did not give Kalindi a moral lecture in return. On the contrary, she felt a genuine sympathy for the situation her friend was in. She even approached the education officer to put a word in for a teacher's job for her in case a suitable vacancy came up. While the officer promised to help, he did not consider a woman of Kalindi's reputation the right person for a schoolteacher's job. The education department would come in for severe censure from all sides if he made such an appointment. However, he said there were other jobs open to qualified women like her where her background would not be a problem. By a strange coincidence, soon after he made a promise to let Esther know if any such job came up, he received a letter from the labour department saying there was a vacancy for a lady, able and willing to work with women living in Mumbai's working-class areas. When she heard about the job from Esther, Kalindi saw it as a ray of hope and instantly decided to apply for it.

It is time to pause here for an introduction to Esther Killekar. Esther lived with her mother. Her father had passed away when she was still a child. Her mother and her uncle—her mother's brother—raised her and saw her through school and college. It helped her uncle that Esther was a very bright student and a regular winner of scholarships. And it helped her mother that the Rasta Peth house in which they lived had been passed down to them as an ancestral legacy. Esther had a brother. He was not as bright as her. Without financial aid through scholarships, he could not go to college as she had done. He trained instead as a fitter, a skill that brought him a job in Burma where he now lived. Consequently there was a very clear difference in class between the sister and brother.

Esther knew most of her neighbours well. She also had friends among Hindus. She was particularly proud that she could speak and write chaste Marathi. She had graduated with Sanskrit as her main subject. That had given her important insights into the Hindu religion and way of life. She was proud to be called a Maharashtrian. She was as yet single, caught between two stools. She was well-educated, which scared off eligible young men from her community who were moderately educated and had average prospects. Those who were highly educated and had better prospects were looking to marry wealthier girls. Thus, while her education gave her a high standing in society, she did not have the wealth to match that status in high society. This often led her to wonder secretly why she should try to find a partner in her own community at all. So, when she met Kalindi after all these years and heard her story, she saw it as a somewhat magical coincidence that it should happen at this point in her own life.

Something else added to the complications in Esther's life. A social upheaval was afoot in her community, which was reflected in the conversations the family had at home. The Bene Israels originally belonged to the Konkan coast of Maharashtra. They bore local surnames like Penkar, Ziratkar and Ashtamkar and had adopted many Hindu customs. But when they moved from the coast to the hinterland and came in contact with European Jews like the Sassoons, they aspired to be seen as coming from the same stock. Consequently, they abandoned their original names to assume European Jewish names like Jacob, Ezekiel and Samson. With the European presence, politically as rulers and socially as 'pure' Jews, a distinct rift divided the Bene Israel community. An attempt was underway to establish their heritage as European. Accident had brought them to the Indian coast. Perhaps only men had arrived first. Without women, they must have co-habited with local women. Centuries later the men of the community regretted the fact that local women had seduced them. This argument angered the women in the community. They said it was not surprising that men should blame women for what they saw as their fall. Adam himself had started the tradition. Women were also angered by the young men of the community trying to get European Jewish girls to marry them. They saw in their sorry efforts their own rejection. The social rift was thus not only vertical, between wealthy families with the means to aspire to European ways and the others unable to do so; but also horizontal between genders with women being less keen than men on adopting Western ways. Western ways meant accepting English as a home language. The trend was to send children to schools where English was the medium of instruction. But only those of a certain class could afford to do this. When children began to study and speak English, they were discouraged from mixing with children who still went to Marathi-teaching schools. Children were thus divided along class and language lines.

Esther's uncle, a barrister in Mumbai, was one of the aspirational Bene Israels whose pro-Western convictions had become stronger during his years in England where he had gone to study. There he had met several Jews and saw for the first time that the Bene Israels were a small branch of a massive tree whose branches spanned the whole of Europe. The community had once been oil-pressers. After they moved out of Konkan, they had become proficient in other trades. Many had acquired higher education and were now practising professionals. It was still a very small community, numbering no more than ten or twelve thousand. But their social weight had increased and Esther's uncle felt they were now in a position to be acknowledged by the larger Jewish community. He had even tried briefly to start a Zionist movement in India which would make the Bene Israels part of the worldwide movement.

He was naturally keen to see at least his family completely Westernized. Towards this end he had persuaded his sister to name her daughter Esther. Now he was trying to persuade the daughter to assume her father's name Isaac or her grandfather's name Shamshun as her surname. Esther had different ideas. She argued privately that if people like her uncle believed European

Jews had accidentally drifted to the west coast of India and married Hindu women, then all Bene Israels must think of themselves as born to Hindu mothers. To reject this vital part of themselves was to insult women and motherhood. Thus, although her uncle had enrolled her in school as Esther Isaac, she preferred to be called Esther Killekar.

It is because of her thoughts on the bond between Bene Israels and Hindus that Esther had begun to wonder why she should not marry a Maharashtrian Hindu. In that sense, both friends were looking for a future. Esther for a husband and Kalindi for a job that would help her stand on her feet.

10. A Heart-to-heart Chat

During the days that followed her coming to stay with Esther, Kalindi spent all her time corresponding with the government department in Mumbai which was finally to offer her a job. Soon the friends returned to their old intimacy and spoke freely about their fears, dreams and desires.

Esther asked, 'What made you leave home to live with a married grocer?'

Kalindi replied by giving her friend a purple pad which contained a sheaf of twenty or twenty-five handwritten pages. 'Here is an explanation, a justification of why I did it.'

Esther glanced at the top sheet. It was a letter. 'To whom is it addressed?'

'To my brother; but in fact, to the whole of Maharashtra.'

'You mean you intended to publish it?'

'Yes. But after my death. In fact I was sure it would be published whether I intended it or not.'

'Are you telling me that you were going to kill yourself?'

'Yes. That was why I got off at Khadakwasla.'

'Why did you have a trunk with you then?'

'I wasn't thinking of death when I boarded the bus. I had bought a ticket to Donje. But I saw the Khadakwasla lake and decided to get off.'

'And you wrote this letter before jumping in.'

'I did.'

'Which means I got there just in time. And did a great good deed entirely by accident.'

'You did indeed.'

'So you have said all you wanted to here, in this letter?'

'Yes. Holding nothing back.'

Esther began to read the letter.

Dear Brother,

When this letter finds you, I, Kalindi, will have quit this world. Please forgive me if I have ever wronged you, which I am certain you will. I have not wronged the world but the world has always looked upon me as a wrongdoer. I am therefore writing down everything that I want the world to know. I would like you to publish this because I want those who knew me and condemned me and those who did not know me and even then condemned me to know what lay in my heart.

I would like all my accusers to ponder over one point. Had a prostitute's daughter taken to prostitution you would not have held her guilty of wrongdoing. But I became a sinner only because I rejected marriage and chose to live with a man for love. Why? The only reason was that I was the daughter of a brahmin.

Yes. I was born to a brahmin; yet I did not receive the opportunities that daughters of brahmins do as a matter of course. Ironically, I did not even have the freedom of conduct that a prostitute's daughter has. My problem was not only that I was born to a brahmin, but that the brahmin I was born to believed caste should be abolished and acted upon his belief by marrying outside his caste.

I have come to the conclusion that every leader who has ever made public statements against the caste system is either dishonest or an ass. All reformists and Prarthana Samaj notables were birds of the same feather. They spent their entire lives parroting the lines they knew by heart without once supporting their words with action. All they did was lure others to their doom. People who heaped praise on these charlatans while they were alive, did so in self-interest. Those men are dead and gone. Turned to ashes. Had it not been so, honest Prarthana Samaj believers of today would have celebrated their anniversaries by digging up their corpses and thrashing them with their slippers. When Prarthana Samaj leaders passed a resolution that all brahmins should cast away their sacred threads, not a single one of them actually did. Only two men did—the Kelkar brothers. When they realized this, one of them did penance to be allowed to wear it again.

In this world, honest people fall prey to the manipulation of cunning men. The cunning move with the wind. The world appears to be made for these crooks. Honest men like my father live to see the disintegration of their families. As regards caste discrimination, I believe nobody should get entangled with the issue. I also believe that nobody should marry as an act of self-sacrifice. Nobody has the right to do

> that. For the person who does so, is not the only one to suffer the consequences. His family must suffer them too. He at least earns praise for his deed. His children do not get even that. All they get is misfortune.

At the end of this diatribe, Kalindi had turned to narrating her own story. We will not reproduce it in its entirety here. We shall excerpt only a few parts.

> I was given a college education which prepared me for a job—one job. Teaching. I did not want to teach. As a matter of fact, I did not think working had any part in my future life. If a woman has been encouraged from childhood to play with dolls and aspire to becoming a mother, how would the idea of working for a living enter her world? But I realized soon enough that the twin dreams of marriage and motherhood would always elude me. I was not looking for a rich husband, but an educated man. No such proposals came my way. Nor could I dream of finding a husband for myself. That would have involved a secret relationship. My father was liberal in some respects; but he disapproved of men and women mingling openly. As a result, very few men came into my life. One of them was Shivsharanappa.
>
> People must wonder how I could have fallen in love with him. He was certainly not the best-looking of men, judged by general standards. I am certain people made wild surmises about why I did it. I would like to say it was not for the reasons they suspected. Although Shivsharan was well-off, his lifestyle was nothing like a barrister's. Moreover, I had no idea at all about his financial condition. I had assumed he stood somewhere

> between being poor and having enough to live on. As it happened, I did not fear poverty. I had seen women from the lowest ranks washing and cleaning for well-off families and living perfectly happy lives. To live off a man's wealth had never been my goal. My aim was to be a companion to my husband, share in his joys and sorrows, support him and give him courage when he was down.
>
> Perhaps I was looking for an unhappy man into whose life I could bring joy! When Shivsharan started dropping me off to college in his car, I became curious about the workings of this machine. I would sit in the passenger seat and ask him many questions. He would answer my questions but also talk about his home and his life. These snatches of conversation gave me the idea that he was a good but unhappy man.

Esther stopped reading at this point and said, 'Your feelings will find an echo in many women. But men will not understand them at all. Most men believe women love them for their virtues or their fortunes. Personally, I too believe that women are more attracted to men who need them than to men who have it all.'

Kalindi was so happy to have found someone who thought and felt as she did, that she got up impulsively and gave Esther a hug.

'So you feel a woman is right to give her heart to a man because he is unhappy?'

'I am not saying what she should or should not do. I am merely saying that is what women do. As for the question should they, the answer depends on how you look at it. Wisdom demands that you look for maximum benefits for yourself. Most people would not advise you to think *only* of material benefits when choosing your mate, but *also* of material benefits.'

'You seem to know a lot about love and marriage. Have you been in love?'

'Come on, Kalindi. You know what we are like. The minute we turn fifteen or sixteen, we feel the stirrings of love in our hearts and we automatically attach ourselves to the nearest male. Sadly, the nearest male is by and large not someone that your parents or the world thinks of as the right one for you. You are supposed to forget those early crushes. And in time you do. Anyway, why link love to marriage?'

'That's a pragmatic woman's philosophy, Esther. But do you actually live according to it?'

'I haven't had the opportunity to test myself yet. I have loved many. I remember being crazy about a tailor who lived next door to us when I was not quite thirteen. Later it was a good-looking fellow who rode a bicycle and delivered newspapers. I am still not married. Perhaps that's the answer to your question.'

'No, it is not. The more educated we are, the higher we aim. If the newspaper boy had proposed to you, would you have accepted him?'

'I might have. But I wouldn't have been allowed to. It was enough that I could receive my newspaper from him. Luckily it was always he who came to deliver it. Had he suspected my feelings and shown the guts to propose to me, I might even have eloped with him. I was about fifteen years old and my young heart was constantly leaping about.'

'How old was he?'

'Twenty-two maybe.'

'So he'd be about thirty-five now.'

'For heaven's sake, Kalindi. Don't start sleuthing.'

'The man who comes to deliver newspapers now is about that age. Is he the man? He's not at all good-looking.'

'It is him. He was really good-looking back then. But life does things to you. His responsibilities have taken a lot out of him. He has three children. I feel nothing for him now. I even wonder why I ever did.'

'So, tell me what kind of man you'd like to marry now. Someone you love or someone who has money?'

'To tell you the truth, I'm at a stage where I will marry any man who will have me. I am twenty-eight. There are no educated bachelors of my age in our community. The educated ones get snapped up fast. What is available now are the uneducated ones. So my choice is either one of them or an educated widower.'

'What's wrong with a man who is less educated?'

'Actually nothing. If educated men can marry uneducated women, why can it not be the other way around? The only problem is that men fear women who are more educated than themselves.'

'That is true too.'

'Your parents' mixed-caste marriage has created problems for you. But you must remember that other women have problems of other kinds. Many pure brahmin women have also fallen behind in the marriage race because of their education.'

'Really?'

'Of course. Many of your graduate batchmates are still single. But let me return to your letter.'

Esther resumed reading the letter:

> Shivsharan would say his wife was not literate. She was extremely narrow minded. Emotions like compassion and fellow-feeling were totally absent in her to the extent that she did not share in either his joys or his sorrows. I decided he was a victim of the cruel custom of child marriage. His father must have married him off when he was a boy and he now found himself trapped in this tragic mismatch. I began to think of his wife as an ogress.

'Had you not met his wife?' Esther asked.

'Read the whole letter first,' Kalindi said.

> I had never seen Shivsharan's wife Thayamma out with him in his car. In fact I had never seen her. Nor had Aai. When she had inquired about her once, Shivsharan had said she was conservative in her ways and preferred not to go out. But I discovered later that that was not the case at all. Thayamma was dark and her face was pitted with pock marks. That is why Shivsharan felt embarrassed to take her out. Despite what he considered her drawbacks, it turned out she was not bad-looking at all. If she dressed well and groomed herself well, she would be very presentable. But since her husband did not care for her, she had stopped caring for herself and ended up looking frumpy. Shivsharan wanted to

be seen in public with good-looking, stylish women. That is why he was always keen to take Aai, Usha and me out for a drive. I failed to see Shivsharan as he really was till things about his life began revealing themselves to me. Earlier I had wondered why, if he was so unhappy in his marriage, he did not divorce his wife. His community allowed him to do that. I realized later that he was not unhappy in his marriage. In fact he even felt what one could call love for Thayamma. So there was no question of his wanting to abandon her. Had I known this, I would never have left home to live with him. I decided to live with him only because I thought I could bring some love and caring into the life of a man who was deprived of both.

There was another reason why I felt this was a way out of the situation that my mixed parentage had placed me in. I had begun to question the very fundamentals of my case. Was I a Hindu? There was evidence to prove I was and society also accepted me as a Hindu. For example, I was not an untouchable like the Mahars were. They were outcasts. They were not Hindu, else they would not have been forbidden from entering the temples of Hindu gods. We were not debarred from temples. That proved we were Hindu. The problem was, to seek marriage, a Hindu had to belong to a caste. I did not. My father thought his children were brahmins. Society disagreed with him. So we were left in limbo. Neither the social laws that governed the lives of untouchables, nor of brahmins applied to us. We were the nowhere people. And so....

That is where the letter ended. Esther asked, 'What were you going to write after this?'

'I have no idea. I was so full of grief then that my ideas were pouring out of me. Somehow I no longer feel that way. I can't remember what I was going to say.'

'You mean you have started feeling so differently now that you don't even recall your sorrows?'

'I can't say I have forgotten that time of total despair. The feeling of instability, of not knowing what the future held, still makes me anxious. If I get a job...'

'You will, Kalindi. I'm sure you'll find a job.'

'How can you be so sure?'

'Don't ask me. I just do. And till you find a job, you are welcome to stay here.'

'That's really kind of you. But I must ask you something. Will someone like me being here not affect your reputation?

'If it does, we'll deal with it. Come to think of it, why do we worry about reputations? For two reasons: we want to hold on to our jobs and we hope to marry.'

'Yes.'

'Well, as far as my job is concerned, I don't need to worry. I have already told my director about you and he himself is looking for an opening for you.'

'And marriage?'

'I'm not going to worry about that. My reputation was unquestionably intact before you came to stay. Did the marriage market welcome me? Had my value there been of any account, then I might have worried about loss of reputation.'

'What is your value according to you?'

'Roughly one paisa—the copper one with a hole. If one half of it is lost, what difference would it make?'

'Esther, you are only making a pretense of being worthless. Actually you are making a sacrifice to help a friend. Don't I see that? Well-educated, good-looking girls like you aren't found at every street corner.'

'Rubbish. Don't attribute noble ideas like sacrifice to me. They belong to the moral brigade at the other end of town. Say at most that I am doing my duty by a friend.'

'You are such a lovely person, Esther. If you haven't been grabbed, it can only be because the men in your community are blind.'

'Then do you know a sighted man from outside my community? Please send him along. Invite him for dinner this evening.'

'I wish I could. But to be honest, I haven't made a single new male acquaintance in the last three years. But tell me something. Your heart has been beating for men since you were thirteen. Are you saying that in all this time it found only a tailor and a newspaper boy to beat for?'

'Who said? I can't count the number of times I fell for a well turned-out man or a good-looking youth.'

'You are talking about two species of male. What do you mean by man and what do you mean by youth?

'A man is someone older than me and a youth is someone younger.'

'Don't tell me you have fallen for younger men!'

'I thought you knew the tricks that hearts can play on you.'

'Well, I don't. Remember I'm a few years younger than you.'

'Age isn't the only reason. The distance that I walked

from here to our school was three times the distance you walked from yours. That means every day I was gaining three times the knowledge of the world than you.'

'You are only putting me off with your flippant answers. I want to know if you didn't ever desire an educated, good-looking man—forget his age.'

'That's better. So here's my story. There was a young man. Yes. I saw him only once. At a cricket match. He was wearing a sports jacket and he dimpled when he smiled.'

'Did you find out his name? Did you have a chance to talk to him?'

'I don't know his name. But I heard his companions call him Aaba. I didn't talk to him. But he picked up my handkerchief, which I had accidentally dropped. I thanked him. That's when he smiled and I noticed his dimple.'

'Esther. Shall I tell you where the match was played? At PYC Gymkhana.'

'That's right. How do you know?'

'I was there. And the young man you are speaking of is my brother Satyavrat. We call him Aaba. And he does have a dimple.'

11. A Woman Has a Question

By a strange coincidence, soon after the friends had spoken to one another about love and marriage, the magazine *Chandrika* came out with a story, written under the assumed name Nayadevbhagini. It purported to be an account of the betrayal of a friend's love. The friend's name, Upendravajra, was also clearly assumed. Intrigued by the illustration that headed the story and its title, 'The Sad Tale of a Young Woman's Betrayal', Esther and Kalindi began reading it instantly. This is how the story went.

> I have long wondered what our society, which stigmatizes young girls for the smallest step they might take off the straight and narrow path which has been laid down for them, expects them to do with their lives thereafter. This question has recently crystallized for me around the life of my friend Upendravajra, who has suffered at the hands of an unconscionable young man and society at large. My story is based on the correspondence she has had with him and the diary entries she made during that time, both of which she has shown me in strictest confidence as proof of her innocence. I do not expect my readers merely to read this story but to mull over

it and respond to my question: What is Upendravajra to do with her life now?

Upendravajra was in her first year at college when she met a senior student, Nanabhai, in the library. She is a friendly soul with a ready smile. They happened to be at the same book case when they met. She was trying to reach for a book on the top shelf of the cupboard. He asked if he could help. She was grateful for the offer. He found the book she wanted. She smiled at him and said thank you. They had nothing more to say to one other and went their separate ways.

One day she received a brief letter in the post signed Nanabhai. The writer reminded her of their meeting in the library and wondered if they could not be friends. It was addressed to her as Sister Upendravajra and begged her not to be offended by his request. The letter confused her. What was the meaning of it? Could a friendship be engineered in this way? Should it not simply happen? How was she to respond? He had seemed a nice enough man and probably meant no harm. She would not like to offend him by not replying to his invitation even if it was to say no thank you. But would writing back be the right thing to do? What did young college girls do in such a case? She had made no friends yet at college with whom she could discuss the problem. If only she could have shown the letter to her father and asked for his opinion. He too was college educated and must have wanted to be friends with girl students in his time. Was this how he or his friends had gone about it? But he would not have answered the question helpfully. Instead, he would have been upset that a male student had dared write to her in the first place and would order her not only not to write back but to cut him dead if he ever attempted to talk to her again.

Knowing this, she did not take her confusion to her father, but continued to think about the problem for herself until she finally concluded that there was no harm in responding to Nanabhai's letter. She made her letter short. Beginning with the greeting 'Dear brother Nanabhai', she assured him that she was not offended by his letter. However, she felt that since they attended the same college, they were likely to run into each other in the library or during college events. When that happened, they could greet each other as friends for she did not hold friendship between young men and women as wrong although many girls believed it to be so. She added that perhaps they themselves did not believe it was wrong but submitted to what their elders and society at large expected them to believe. She signed off as 'Your sister, Upendravajra'. She received a reply by return of post in which Nanabhai thanked her for not taking offence and said he looked forward to running into her soon.

Upendravajra now thinks Nanabhai engineered the next meeting and the ones that followed and suddenly she found herself complicit in a friendship that necessarily had to be secret. Inevitably she had begun to feel drawn to him and he to her. After each 'accidental' meeting she would receive a letter from him to say how much it had meant to him to spend a few precious minutes with her. Somewhere during that time, she noticed that he had stopped addressing her as sister. First it became 'dear' and then 'dearest Upendravajra'.

Although she did not address him as dearest, she too had dropped the fig leaf of 'brother'.

In reply to one of his letters, she pointed out that their friendship was drawing attention in the college and they should stop meeting one another in public places like the library. She suggested that he should meet her on her walks by the canal where no young people walked. He was delighted at the suggestion. He must have kept a watch on her because she did not walk regularly nor at a set time. But whenever she was out, he was there to join her. They had a lot to talk about and discuss, the college being a source of news as well as gossip. On one of these evenings, when they happened to be on a quiet path off the main road, he put his arms around her and kissed her. She was taken aback. She told him off in no uncertain terms and walked home in confusion and anger. The very next day she received a letter from him that was full of the deepest of apologies. His only excuse for his behaviour was the deep love he had developed for her. She could not really hold that against him, could she? For surely, she too felt the same way about him. However, he realized that, given their society, they should not express their love in the fashion in which he had done. He ended the letter by once again asking her to forgive him. She thought over his letter and decided that an impetuous young man might very well make such a mistake. She should not hold it against him especially since it was the result of love and nothing harmful. So she wrote back forgiving him. He was happy to be forgiven. But when excited, his emotions refused to be reined in. One day he could not contain himself. He made a worse mistake than the earlier one. This time he appeared to be bent on stealing her virginity.

This time when he wrote a letter of apology, she did not respond. He wrote several more letters, always apologizing but always offering the same excuse. It was his extreme love for her that had driven him to the act. Surely, she could not hold that against him?

Although she was very angry at the attempt he had made to force himself on her, she allowed herself to think about it from his point of view. She told herself that women were more bound by societal rules than men. Men were more used to giving vent to their emotions because they ran fewer risks in doing so. Was she denying that the emotion of love was powerful enough to drive a man to the act that he had nearly committed? The question caused her to examine her own feelings. Gradually she realized that she was as attracted to him physically as he was to her. The only difference was that she had greater self-control than him. If a lack of self-control was his only weakness, perhaps they could find a solution for it. As it happened, his next letter contained the solution. He wrote, 'If I am too weak to control my emotions when we meet, let me remove the temptation itself. Let us not meet as we have been doing in private places. It was necessary to do so to give us time to express ourselves to each other. Those meetings have served to bring us close. We have grown to know each other. It is important for us now to build on this friendship. Let us return to our public meetings in the library. I hope you will agree that this would solve our problem. Remember, I cannot rest until you have forgiven me and we can meet again.'

Upendravajra replied immediately saying, 'Although the idea of platonic love was not born in Hindustan, I am sure many men and women in our country have experienced it. The great historian V.K. Rajwade has said that Bayabai's love for Swami Ramdas, one of our greatest saints, was of this nature—platonic. This is the first day of the year 1926. What could be more joyful than our starting the new year with a new commitment to friendship?'

At the end of that year, Nanabhai appeared for his final examination and passed. The question of his future now loomed before him. He decided to go to a law college in Mumbai. Since his father could not support him, he was going to try and pay his way. The two friends had now begun to talk of marriage. He was of the opinion that he needed to earn well to even think of it. She thought otherwise. She said love was enough to help them live happily even in straitened circumstances. She could find a teaching job and add to their monthly income. She agreed, however, that it had to be his decision since he would be the chief bread-winner. He decided that they should wait.

Nanabhai passed his Bachelor of Law examination in two years, supporting himself with a private tuition that brought him twenty-five rupees a month. Upendravajra continued with her college studies feeling terribly sorry all the while for the conditions in which he had to live. With a degree under his belt, Nanabhai finally found a proper job as a clerk in a solicitor's firm earning one hundred rupees a month. She asked if it wasn't time now for them to marry. Nanabhai was still reluctant. His job as a clerk held no prospects. What would set him on the path to promotion was to find a position as an articled clerk. That would allow him to think of marriage. In order to become an articled clerk, he needed further qualifications.

Nanabhai's letters were now full of the crooked ways of the legal profession which he was experiencing first hand. He wrote in particular about the Clientele Secretary who knew the ins and outs of every scandal in Mumbai. 'This man has assured me that there is no obstacle at all to my becoming an articled clerk. He has promised to make arrangements for the money I will require to become a solicitor, a prerequisite for an articleship. Some of this man's ways make me uncomfortable. But I have to admit that he is very clever.'

Nanabhai also wrote to her about a Parsi woman who wanted to divorce her husband for infidelity. She came to the office armed with evidence. Her story was that there were unoccupied houses on Nepean Sea Road where gardeners were appointed as caretakers. If you wanted to have a few hours of privacy for a liaison, you could bribe a gardener to allow you to 'view' the house for a few hours as a prospective buyer. She had proof that her husband was using the services of a gardener to spend time with his lady love in one of these houses. Nanabhai's boss asked her, salaciously, how she knew about these hideouts. She said without hesitation that during her long engagement with her husband, they had found it very difficult to hold back physically. Her husband had often taken her to one of these bungalows. Nanabhai's boss asked her, pretending that it would help him build her case, 'Didn't you suspect his moral character then?' To this she replied, 'How would that have helped? Suppose I had suspected him and asked him questions, and suppose he had come out with the truth that he had often taken young women there, I would have had to break off the engagement out of self-respect. That would not have helped me at all, because breaking the engagement would have reduced my prospects of finding another suitor to nil. I thought it better not to ask and proceed with the engagement.'

Nanabhai wrote that he was at first vastly amused with the woman's frank defence of herself; but that later he saw where the root of the problem lay. 'People get into long engagements because they are waiting for the man to study till he is qualified for a job that will bring enough money for the couple to live well. During the years that intervene between engagement and marriage it is natural for young people to want to give in to their physical desires. Why should we judge them for doing what is natural? They are victims of social circumstances.'

Upendravajra was put off by the tone of these letters. She demanded to know in her reply whether the instances he spoke of created feelings of revulsion or amusement in him. She questioned her own feelings and remembered that she and Nanabhai too had been trapped by similar circumstances leading them to cease meeting each other privately. It was perhaps right that Nanabhai did not judge the woman he spoke of, harshly.

Suddenly after this, Nanabhai stopped writing long letters to Upendravajra. All she received were picture postcards with a few lines that spoke of his love for her. She asked him whether he was too busy to write and asked how much longer he had decided they should wait before marrying. He wrote back to say the Clientele Secretary was making arrangements for his promotion and as soon as that came through, he would begin to earn enough for them to marry. Then there was silence again. When Upendravajra next asked about his plans for marriage he wrote a letter in which he claimed he had never promised to marry her. If she had kept all his letters, she could check back and see if he had said, in any of them, that he would marry her. All he had said repeatedly was that he loved her. And that, he wrote, was still true.

She wrote to him instantly demanding to know whether the money that the Clientele Secretary had said he could arrange for him involved his marrying a rich woman. It turned out that her guess was right. The solicitor's firm for which Nanabhai was working had once hushed up an affair between a rich young woman and a rake. When the time came for her family to marry her off, the solicitor had mediated a deal whereby the rake had been paid off. Additionally the Clientele Secretary had promised to find her a respectable groom who had come to Mumbai from Pune and would not have heard of the affair. The young man was in need of money. If the girl's family gave him a handsome dowry, she would win herself a husband.

My question to you dear readers is this: What should Upendravajra do now? She is heart-broken. The man whom she trusted most has betrayed her. Now if she wishes to marry, what should she do? Hide the truth from her prospective groom thus cheating him? She is too honest a girl to do that. The alternative is for her

> to confess to her previous affair. In that case, do my readers feel there is a single young man in our society who will take her earlier behaviour as natural and totally human and not hold it against her?'

Kalindi and Esther, and as it happened Satyavrat, too, waited for readers to respond. He too had read the story and for a brief while wondered if it had not been written by his sister. But none of the details of the story matched the details of her wrongdoing which society had found worthy of even greater condemnation. He was intrigued by the question that the writer had posed at the end. It was going to throw everybody into a dilemma. On the one hand, they would be expected to uphold the cause of truth. If they wrote in favour of the woman telling her prospective suitor the truth, the question that would automatically follow would be, are you therefore condemning a young woman to lifelong spinsterhood because a young man of good family thought nothing of deceiving her? Or are you saying there are enough respectable, educated young men around who will be willing to marry her despite the false step she had taken?

Since the readers could not confront the challenge the writer had thrown to society head-on, they sidestepped the issue altogether. Several articles were written questioning whether the writer was a woman at all. The conclusion they arrived at was that the writer was a man. That seemed to settle the issue for them. One reader decided the 'story' was not based on facts. It was probably a translation of an English story, for it was not our culture for women to step outside the house and go for walks freely with young men. An editorial in another magazine pointed out that this story was proof of the terrible effects modern education was having on young women. Yet another stated categorically and with a high degree of disgust that such stories were the result of girls being allowed to stay single to an advanced age. The story had done an excellent job of showing how this practice resulted in young people getting acquainted with each other and falling out of step with society.

Kalindi and Esther on their side and Satyavrat on his were equally angry at these responses. Kalindi said to Esther, 'I wish Aaba was with us. We used to discuss such things very often. We saw how many educated men who pretended to be reformists were actually cowards who stood with the herd. My father was mistaken in his understanding of the world. But at least he did what he spoke of. He married a woman from a lower caste. I wonder what he would say about this story.'

Although most readers and editors had sidestepped the question that Nayadevbhagini had asked, one reader wrote a response which appeared in the next issue of *Chandrika*. The story was autobiographical and was signed 'Unlucky or Lucky?' The story went like this.

Dear Nayadevbhagini,

I have no idea how society will answer the question you have posed but I give here my experience which shows that it is not only women who are treated unfairly by men. Men too get unfair treatment from women. When the question arises of whether to tell the truth or omit to tell it to the woman the jilted man proposes to marry, he faces exactly the same dilemma as the woman in your story. Like Upendravajra, I too had given my heart to a young woman. When I arrived in Mumbai looking for work, I was engaged by Manoharlal, a rich merchant, to tutor his son, Mansukhlal. I was paid twenty-five rupees a month to teach him for one hour a day. Mansukhlal was in his final year at school but knew practically nothing of the subjects he had to study. He had never passed in any of them but had been promoted each year because Manoharlal was on the school committee. But the school had no such powers when it came to the matriculation examination. Manoharlal insisted that the son pass the exam. I explained the problem to him. The only solution was to keep him from school and for me to teach him all the subjects for at least three hours every day. There was a chance then that he would be ready to appear for his matriculation in six months.

Manoharlal was happy with the idea. He increased my pay to fifty rupees and I became financially independent. Later my salary was increased to sixty because Manoharlal requested me to teach Mansukhlal's older sister Karunasundari as well. She was twenty-one years old and had been given no formal education. She had no interest in studying mathematics. What she wanted to learn was Sanskrit and English. So after teaching Mansukhlal for three hours, I would teach her for one hour. My tuition would occupy the entire afternoon. I spent my mornings studying law.

Karunasundari was engaged to a man a few years younger than her. The community to which Manoharlal belonged was so small that it was difficult to find a groom who would suit her. Both families had thought it fit to let him grow a little older before they married. Now this young woman had been writing poems and stories for many years before I started teaching her. To begin with only one magazine published her work. Manoharlal had assured the publisher that he would pick up a hundred copies of every issue in which her writing appeared. He was very proud of her. He himself had no education. Although he was wealthy, he was not part of cultured society. His daughter's writing was published, liked, discussed. This gave him the place that he aspired for in society. By the time I entered the household, Karunasundari's writings had begun to appear in other magazines too. With the smattering of Gujarati I had picked up, I managed to read one of her stories and realized it was plagiarized from an old film. But meanwhile I had begun to feel attracted towards her. So I praised the story. Soon, besides being her tutor, I became her first reader, critic and mentor.

This was a position of responsibility but also an opportunity for greater intimacy. Then came casual questions from her about my private life. Have you never been in love? It would not have been honourable for me to ask her the same question. But I did feel that her question indicated that she had developed a personal interest in me. She used to wear blouses that left her neck exposed. The sight of her neck excited me. But naturally I resisted the temptation of touching it. However, one day she playfully put her hand in my pocket. Another day she tickled me. She was twenty-one years old. I could not put these actions down to innocent playfulness. They had to mean something more. One day I ventured to lay my hand on her neck. She let it lie there for a while. That was a sign that she was not offended. After that our love-making proceeded as you would expect it to till it culminated in an act which was the furthest we could have gone under the circumstances.

The next day I gave her a gift, an expensive sari, that would normally have cost fifty rupees but which I had managed to get for twenty-five. This was a rich sari compared to the three- or four-rupee saris that Karun generally wore. She showed the sari to her mother who said I should not have spent so much on the gift. Karun was extremely pleased with it. In my mind I saw her dressed in it and felt even closer to her. A few days later I asked her when we could marry. She said, 'Please don't talk about marriage so soon.'

I thought that was fair. So I gave her more time. When I asked her again a few months later, she told me quite frankly that marriage with me was out of the question. That is when, for the first time, she spoke of her engagement. Surely you can break it I said. How can you marry your fiancé now that you love me? She explained to me that love was one thing and marriage another. She had been given gold ornaments worth twenty thousand rupees when she got engaged. I said surely she could return them. In time I would give her more gold than that. She laughed and said I'd be an old man by then and she would be past the age when she enjoyed wearing ornaments.

Then she grew serious and said, 'How can I break off my engagement? That would be betraying my fiancé and his family. My father too would suffer a grave loss.'

'How is that?' I asked.

'Every time he needs money, he goes to my father-in-law for it.'

I understood now that she had been leading me on. Nor did she appear to feel any shame.

She spoke to her mother about it. Her mother also laughed and said, 'Teacher, our Karun regards you as her older brother. How can you think of marrying her? Anyway, you are a brahmin. There are so many beautiful, well-educated girls in your caste. Why do you want to ruin your life by marrying a Baniya girl?'

I had no answer to give. I was deeply disturbed. I wondered if I had been dishonourable in making love to a woman who was engaged to another man. The more I thought about it the less guilty I felt on that account. I would not have done what I did had I known about the engagement. I did not go to Manoharlal's house for four days after that. But I went on the fifth. Did my duty by teaching Mansukh and Karun. The more I thought about my situation, the less I respected Karun. I have now got over the humiliation of that period of my life. But my question to Nayadevbhagini is the same as hers to her readers. Do I tell the woman I ultimately marry the truth about Karun or not? To my mind it is best that the girl in her story not reveal the truth just as I will not. What we need to do is to be true to the people we marry and win their trust completely. Neither of us has erred. If we have, it was for love. Let us not blame ourselves. Let us put these painful episodes behind us, erase them from our minds and make healthy and happy lives for ourselves.

After they read this story, Kalindi and Esther decided the storyteller's conclusion was not completely convincing for one reason. If the truth about Upendravajra's liaison ever came out, she would never be forgiven by either society or her husband. If Unlucky or Lucky's misadventure was revealed, society would forgive him for being what men are and are allowed to be. His wife might feel some misgivings but would not dare blame him because, being dependent on him, she would only harm herself if she did. The writer still does not know that the balance is already weighted on his side.

12. Kalindi Leaves Pune

Kalindi finally received her appointment letter for a job in Mumbai and a sea change came over her. She no longer felt like an abandoned woman or a social outcast. Instead, she realized that, if she had not been found fit for a certain kind of life, that of a married woman, it was because she was fit for another kind of life. She felt that everything in her adult life—all the ups and downs, the fears and doubts—had been leading to this conclusion. She had been meant all along for a life of independence. The idea that she was going to earn her living was accompanied by the thought that nobody would now have the right to give her unwanted advice about how to lead her life and how to value herself. If anybody attempted to humiliate her, she would tell them without hesitation that she knew exactly what she was worth.

Marriage? What use was it if it was not to give her son respectability? His education would have suffered had she continued living with the uneducated Shivsharanappa. She had once found it difficult to make even twenty-five rupees a month. She was now going to earn one hundred and fifty. With that, she could give her son the best education available. He could be a doctor, an engineer, or anything else he chose. She could even send him to England. 'There is no reason now to care either about Shivsharanappa or even my father and mother who treated me like some low creature not worthy of their station in life.' That was how she began to regard those she had once loved.

With all that it must be said, although Kalindi was about to start a new life in Mumbai, she was leaving her heart behind in Pune. She had decided to leave the most important person in her life, Chintamani, behind with Esther. She was not worried about him because Esther's mother had grown very fond of him and he of her. What pained her was not to have him with her in her new life. Of course it was just as well. She had no idea what that life was going to be like and whether she would have the time and help to look after him.

There was something else she wished she had been able to accomplish before leaving Pune. She did not care whether she saw her parents or not; but she did want very much to meet Satyavrat. She wondered why he had never come to meet her when she had hit rock bottom and had written to him for support. She had shared a deep bond with him before she left home. She had found him to be a kindred soul. They had had long discussions about society. They had agreed that it was people like them who needed to take a lead in the movement because they had experienced how social divisions created by the caste system affected the psychology of those who were treated as worthless by the upper castes. The low esteem they were granted by society and their consequent belief that they were indeed of little worth, would certainly affect the strength of the nation-in-the-making. Kalindi recalled the times when the two of them attended lectures by reformists on the grounds of the Deccan Sabha. Before going she would say to Satyavrat, 'What can these knuckleheads tell us about caste discrimination? They will begin by assuring us that caste discrimination has absolutely no support in the shastras and end by concluding that the time has come for inter-marriage among the Konkanastha, Deshastha and Karhade brahmins! These people are in reality quite ignorant. They do not even know the first principles of the sociology of nationalization.' On their way home from these lectures, Satyavrat was forced to grant that Kalindi had been absolutely right.

With her departure for Mumbai happening the very next day after her appointment letter arrived, she had no time to get in touch with Satyavrat. Suddenly she felt the need to ask and get answers for all the questions that had lain dormant in her mind. There had been time then to mull over them and wait for an opportunity to meet Satyavrat and find answers to them from him. Esther saw that her friend was very disturbed and when she learned the reason, she assured Kalindi that she would try to discover answers to some at least of her questions. She knew that Kalindi's sister Usha was at Hujur Paga, their old school. She promised to talk to her and find a way of visiting Kalindi's home and perhaps of meeting Satyavrat too if she could.

Kalindi said, 'Please do it. And if you do manage to meet Satyavrat, I give you full permission to pinch his cheeks.'

To which Esther said, 'I don't need a bribe to track him down. It will be my pleasure.'

Talking about her family to Esther, Kalindi had once said, 'My father is a good man. Unfortunately, he has taken on the burden of trying to get his family into the brahmin caste by the back door. He has had enough proof that our society does not work that way; but he finds it very difficult to abandon his great idea of brahminizing our society by including all castes in it.' This had led to a longer discussion about caste and about the social organization of Hindus. Esther realized how marginal her community was. She felt a sense of deprivation that she could not participate in the life of this larger community, which was an ocean to the pond that the Bene Israels lived in.

Reviewing her own position vis-a-vis the family, Kalindi wondered if it was not her supposed wrongdoing but the condition of poverty she had landed herself in that had kept them away from her. After all, her mother had visited her, albeit surreptitiously, when her son was born. It was a time when her circumstances had been comfortable enough for her to have engaged the services of a European nurse. Her mother had shown her great love then. Why not when she had needed that love even more? If caste was one factor, money was another. Once women began to earn their living, they would automatically rise in society's and their own esteem. Women were not going to become financially independent overnight. But it was a goal that Satyavrat and she must include in their aims when they came together to start their movement.

As Kalindi packed to leave for Mumbai, Esther said

to her, 'Don't talk to the people in your compartment. Our people are very curious. They will bombard you with questions about who you are, where you are going, are you married or not, do you have children, how many and so forth. I suggest you arm yourself with a newspaper and don't look up from it. If, despite that, your fellow travellers do catch you in a moment of inattention, prepare a false story about who you are.' Kalindi decided she was going to be a Telugu brahmin called Mrs Appa and set about putting together other biographical details to counter questions with.

Esther came to the station to see Kalindi off. Like her friend, Kalindi too was not wearing a kumkum mark on her forehead. This had aroused the curiosity of the people in Kalindi's compartment. They had watched intrigued when the two young women waved their handkerchiefs in farewell as the train pulled out of the station. As soon as Esther disappeared from view, Kalindi plunged into her copy of the *Times of India* although, having a window seat, she would have dearly loved to soak in the beauty of the passing countryside with its hills and trees. Kalindi loved nature and had even been inspired to write lyrics about it, one of which got published too. Unfortunately, all she got to soak up was the day's news.

When the train stopped at Khadki, more people entered the compartment. The people who had embarked at Pune and caught the best seats began to quarrel with the newcomers who were crowding them out. Luckily, some people got off at Talegaon and the atmosphere in the compartment became friendlier. Kalindi was reading her paper but could not resist glancing out of the window occasionally to admire the forests and hills they were passing. As Esther had predicted, one of her co-passengers, an elderly man who had been eyeing her inquisitively, caught her between her two preoccupations and asked to borrow her newspaper. She gave it to him. That was the opportunity some of the passengers had been waiting for. An elderly woman asked her, 'Where are you going? Mumbai?'

'Yes.'

'Where do you live in Mumbai?'

'I will look for a place when I get there.'

'Are you on your own?'

'Yes.'

The fact that she was not wearing kumkum meant one of two things. Either she was a Christian or she was a widow.

'What is your name?'

'Mrs Appa.'

'What caste would that be?'

'Brahmin.'

'Your first name?'

'Rose.'

'That doesn't sound like a Brahmin name. It is an English word.'

'But that is my name. Like Gulab, which comes from Persian.'

'Who gave you the name? Your parents?'

'No. My father-in-law.'

'So what was your maiden name?'

'Akka.'

'What was your husband's profession?'

'He was a student.'

'Where?'

'In Calcutta.'

'Was he a Bengali?'

'No. A Telugu brahmin like me.'

'So what will you do in Mumbai?'

'I have a job.'

'In the education department?'

'No. In the Secretariat.'

'Your salary?'

'One hundred and fifty rupees.'

The sum she mentioned caused everybody to exchange looks.

'Are you a graduate?'

'No. I dropped out in the final year of college.'

'Which college was that?'

'Bethuen College.'

'It's not a name we have heard.'

'It's in Calcutta. That's where I was educated.'

Kalindi had had enough. She looked at the old man who had borrowed her newspaper and asked for it back. When she leaned over to take the paper, she noticed a man sitting in a corner who had not asked her a single question. He was reading a book. She stole a glance at the book. It was a Labour Office publication. When the train stopped at Lonavala, he got off to buy a couple of newspapers and offered her one. She accepted it gratefully.

They had passed Lonavala and Khandala. The train was

to reverse at Bor Ghat. The Tatas were building a tunnel there that would allow trains to go straight through without reversing. The young man told Kalindi he had visited the site to see the work. She asked him if he worked with the labour department.

'No.'

'I asked because you were reading a publication of that department.'

'That's because I am a secretary in the labour union office.'

'Which union?'

'Textile mills. The workers now realize the importance of joining a union. Unions are growing in strength.'

Kalindi asked no further questions. She did not even ask him his name. She merely made a mental note that, sooner or later, her work would bring her in contact with this young man.

13. Shivsharanappa

So far, we have not met Shivsharanappa directly. All we know of him is his conduct towards Kalindi. We know that Kalindi lived with him in love and trust, that they had a son together, that later he neglected both her and him, brought her to a stage of hunger and starvation and ruined her completely. We have therefore judged him as something of a cad. A stone-hearted man. But if we take his side of the story into account, we might not judge him so harshly. We might find it difficult to decide which parts of his actions were caused by the circumstances in which he found himself trapped, and which were the result of flaws in his character. But first it is important to find out the problems he had to face on account of his relationship with Kalindi.

Shivsharanappa's problems were twofold, both caused by his relationship with Kalindi. The first was the rejection he suffered at the hands of his community who closed ranks against him for what he had done. His community were not merely people he was related to by blood or socially. His community were, like him, tradesmen with whom he had business relations. Ordinarily this would have meant a give-and-take relationship during difficult times. When they ostracized him, that vital connection was cut.

The other and more serious problem was the result of the vast amounts of time he was spending with Kalindi. This was time he should have devoted to his shop, keeping an eye on his workers, his clients and his accounts. As days went by and his long absences continued, his clerk and workers realized they could do more or less as they pleased. If the boss was not around to acknowledge the good work they did in his interests, why look after his interests at all? The bond between boss and worker is not based on ethical principles but on what each can get out of the other.

As a matter of fact, Mallikarjun, his clerk, the chief culprit in bringing about his near ruin, often amused the community by holding forth on how the foundation for a new business was laid. When the community heard the news of a fellow-businessman having lost all, Mallikarjun would smile knowingly and launch forth on his business analysis.

'A merchant's clerk doesn't get the kind of salary a government servant gets. Twenty-five or thirty rupees a month is the going salary. Thirty-five is hitting the ceiling. Forty? Only a madman will pay you that. So what can you put aside from such a paltry sum? Is it possible to put by enough to make up the capital for your own business? Banks could loan you the money. But do they? Try going to one. They want to know how many government securities you have or how much gold. Go to a private money-lender and he says show me your land. So, if a clerk is to start something of his own, he has two options: he gambles or he scalps someone. Who is that someone? Obviously the boss. A clerk looks forward to three strokes of luck. The first is the boss dies and his son or grandson is too young to take over his business. The second is the boss dies and the business falls into the hands of his young and innocent wife. The third is the boss turns out to be an addict or bone lazy. How do you think today's big merchants became big? I know a few cases first hand where the business was founded on a lack of honesty in their dealings when they were clerks.'

When his listeners asked him if he was not a believer in the saying that the British had handed them gratis—Honesty is the best policy—he would look hurt and assert that he did indeed believe in the maxim and would instantly hold forth on this new angle to the problem.

'What is honesty for? It is to gain people's trust. Why is it important to gain people's trust? Because it brings profits in the future. The idea is to be so honest for so long that you are trusted and given the opportunity to betray that trust and make yourself a pile on which to found your own business. So how does the policy of honesty work here? The policy is used in the interests of self-advancement. That is what English education teaches us. National education doesn't teach us any different. It teaches us to get the dead boss's son to sign a deed turning the business into a National Trust instituted for the national good. Once he does that, you don't need to show him the accounts. If he insists on seeing them, he must go to court. There you frame him for planning to murder you. He has no proof that he was never planning to murder you. In the end he commits suicide. It is the birthright of every clerk to ruin his boss and benefit by it.'

Mallikarjun's exposition of a clerk's duties and rights would cause bursts of amusement among his listeners. But it also persuaded his listeners that he was in reality an honest man. A crook was hardly likely to lay bare the strategies of crooked men. Unfortunately for him, Mallikarjun had so far failed to benefit by his own business principles. He had been waiting patiently for the day a chink appeared in his boss's business that he could enter and expand till the whole structure gave way. He had been robbed of such an opportunity once when Shivsharanappa's father had died. That golden opportunity to make a killing had been snatched from him by the presence of the dead man's wife's brother in the house. He was not only too sharp to diddle in business but had cut off Mallikarjun's other possible path to riches by keeping an eagle eye on his sister, making it impossible for Mallikarjun to seduce her.

Mallikarjun was senior to Shivsharan in years and business knowhow. Just when he had given up all hope of putting both advantages to good use, Shivsharan had taken that fatal leap into an extra-marital relationship with Kalindi. Suddenly the chink he had been looking for presented itself before him as a wide-open door through which he swaggered in and set to work. At the end of the year during which Shivsharanappa had remained absent from work and spent lavishly on Kalindi, he was informed by his workers that the merchandise he had ordered had arrived but according to the clerk there was no money in the till to pay for it.

It was then that Shivsaharan woke up as if from a dream and fell straight into a nightmare. Wherever he looked, whomsoever he asked, what he heard and saw told him that he was on the brink of bankruptcy. He had been plundered in every possible way. Merchants he had strictly instructed his people never to give goods on credit to, had been given goods in exchange for bribes. There were precisely fifty rupees in the till with which you could not have stocked even half a sack of chickpeas leave alone a shop full of goods. He asked his Kutchi fellow-merchants for a temporary loan, but they refused to give him a single paisa. He went through the accounts in detail to find out where all his money had gone. The books told him he was owed one lakh rupees while he owed seventy-five thousand rupees. This meant he was not in the red. All he had to do was to recover his dues, pay off his debts and start his business afresh with twenty-five thousand rupees as new capital. He went to his debtors one by one and pressed them hard for what they owed him. At the end of ten or twelve days, he had recovered just about six thousand rupees which had to go straight to his creditors. Consequently, he could not pay his workers their salaries.

Next, Shivsharanappa went to inspect his godown where some goods should still have been stored. There were none now. The place was bare. He noticed that the storekeeper was new. Mallikarjun told him the old one had been stealing stuff and selling it off, so he had got rid of him and appointed another. When Shivsharan asked why he had not been informed about it, Mallikarjun's answer was, 'You came to the office so seldom that I could not give you an account of everything that had happened in your absence.'

Shivsharan tracked down the old storekeeper who was now working for another merchant. He questioned him about stealing from the godown. The man said he had not stolen anything. In fact he had tried to meet him to alert him about what was going on but was turned away by his gatekeeper. Shivsharan discovered that the new storekeeper was Mallikarjun's man. He also discovered that his own gatekeeper had been bribed by Mallikarjun to not allow the old storekeeper in. The old storekeeper reported how the goods were stolen from the godown. What went into the books as goods sold was only a fraction of the goods that were actually given to the buyer. The old storekeeper said, 'I was terribly afraid that when you found out what had happened, you would hold me guilty of theft. I was very happy to lose my job.'

Shivsharan set about in earnest recovering the money owed to him but managed to get back only twenty-five thousand rupees. He lost the remaining fifty thousand. After paying back his creditors he still owed twenty thousand rupees. His godown should have held goods worth forty thousand rupees. What remained was worth just about ten thousand. No new moneys were expected. He was bankrupt. He could not take Mallikarjun to court because he would not want the world to know how totally cleaned out he was. His future business depended on people thinking he had lost a lot but was still solvent. The only way he could make a recovery was to mortgage the bungalow in which Kalindi had been living. The money-lender to whom he mortgaged the bungalow as guarantee for a loan of ten thousand rupees, charged seventy-five rupees interest per month. Shivsharan told him he could rent out the bungalow and use that as the interest on his loan. The money-lender argued that he could only charge twenty-five rupees as rent because the bungalow was located on the outskirts of the town from where his tenant had to take a tonga to get to work which cost him fifty rupees a month. Shivsharanappa was forced to pay fifty rupees per month as interest on the loan.

Shivsharanappa then did what he had to with Mallikarjun. He sacked him. But Mallikarjun had already made enough of a pile to set up his own business. He also found extra satisfaction in the knowledge that he had left Shivsharanappa in a state from which he would find it next to impossible to recover.

When Kalindi set off for Mumbai, Shivsharanappa was still telling himself that he would be back in business soon. That is where we will leave him for the moment.

14. First Days in Mumbai

Esther had written to a family she knew in Mumbai asking them to take Kalindi in as a lodger. It was a Bene Israel family of three women, a widow named Sarah Ashtamkar and her two daughters. They lived in Mazagaon. One daughter was a nurse and the other a schoolteacher. Between them they brought home two hundred and twenty-five rupees. To begin with, the family felt awkward to eat meat and fish at the same table as Kalindi, knowing her to be vegetarian. When she realized this, she assured them that her vegetarianism did not mean that people eating meat at the same table as her was offensive to her. This set their minds at rest and Kalindi settled down very well with them.

The day after she arrived in Mumbai, Kalindi reported to the Labour Office where she was instructed about the nature of her work. It turned out that, in order to gauge the exact circumstances of workers' lives, she would have to visit their homes to find out how much they earned and how much they spent. Only women had been appointed for this work since workers' wives ran their homes and had a more precise knowledge of household expenses. When their visits for the day were done, they had to return to the office and enter the figures for every household in columns on large sheets of paper. Other officers would use these figures to compile statistics, which would reveal the general standard of living of the working class. The neighbourhood of Parel was assigned to Kalindi for her share of the work. When the excitement of having a job and the newness of the work faded, she began to be appalled by the squalor in which workers lived. Even as she was getting used to visiting their homes every day, an incident occurred which shocked her even more and gave her reason to be both apprehensive and cautious for herself in the future.

One day she had come downstairs from the tenement she had visited to find that the tonga, which she had engaged to take her from one part of the area to another, had vanished. A little boy was just telling her that somebody had paid him off and asked him to go when a man turned up and began talking to her in some agitation. He told her that her tonga driver had gone away for a little while to feed his horse and would be back soon. He said he was a schoolteacher and was merely conveying to her the suspicions that the residents of his tenement felt about her visits. Why was the government interested in finding out what they ate and drank? Was it so that they could levy taxes on their food and drink? They had no trust at all in the government's intentions and he would urge her to come to his room and explain the whys and wherefores of what she was doing so that he could put everybody's mind at rest on that score. His room was on the third floor.

When they arrived there, he began pressing her to have mithai. He held the box out to her saying he had bought the mithai specially for her. His tone and look made her thoroughly uncomfortable. She got up instantly and went out to the verandah. When she tried to walk towards the staircase, he grabbed her hand. She jerked it away looking around for an escape. Fortunately, she heard footsteps on the staircase. Next moment the young man she had met on the train came into view. 'I need your help,' she said in as calm a voice as she could muster. 'Can you escort me down to the street please?' The 'teacher' had stepped back into the shadow of his room fearing the disclosure she would surely make. But all she wanted was to escape.

The young man from the train not only hailed a tonga for her but got into it with her. He was going to his office in Poybawadi anyway, right next to her tram stop. He pointed out his office to her. She thanked him for having arrived in time to save her. This time she asked him his name. He said, 'They call me lawyer Ramrao around these parts.' Then added as he walked her to the tram stop, 'If you ever need any help from me, please don't hesitate to ask.' They stood on the pavement for a while talking till the tram arrived. Kalindi boarded the tram to go home.

15. Esther Keeps Her Promise

Esther knew how disturbed Kalindi was before she left Pune. Leaving her previous life behind, she had looked for some assurance that she had once belonged to that life. That assurance would have come from her brother Satyavrat. She had no expectations of her mother. If she had any love in her heart at all for her daughter, it was submerged under the social anxiety she had inherited from her husband. Her sister Usha was still too young to decide the rights and wrongs of Kalindi's choices independently. Satyavrat had always been the one with whom she could have long discussions, occasionally even disagreeing with him, although most times they agreed about the social and moral issues they discussed. So why had he not met her during the time of her abandonment? She had requested Esther to seek him out and find out the reason for his holding aloof from her.

Esther took her promise to her friend seriously. She sent word to Kalindi's mother through her sister Usha, who was in her final year at their old school Hujur Paga, that she would like to visit. Shantabai agreed to the meeting only because she could find no reason to refuse to meet

Esther. Usha was present at the meeting. She introduced Esther to her mother and, after a few formal exchanges, Shantabai asked Esther the purpose of her visit.

'I thought you would like to know about Kalindi's whereabouts,' Esther said.

Shantabai could hardly say she felt no such curiosity with regard to her older daughter. As a matter of fact, since news of her was coming to her unasked, she was more than ready to welcome it.

'Yes, indeed. I would like to know how she is doing.'

Esther told her that Kalindi had left Shivsharanappa a month-and-a-half ago; that she had been staying with Esther after that; that she had been trying to find a job; that she had finally found one in Mumbai; that she had recently left Pune to take up the job and was now earning one hundred and fifty rupees a month.

'And her son? Where is he?' Shantabai asked.

'For the time being he is with me.'

'How could she have left him with you?'

'Did she have an alternative? Her family had abandoned her. I was the only person she could turn to during the terrible circumstances she found herself in.'

'She had only herself to blame for it.'

'A human being can make a mistake. But surely the family should support her when she needs them? Do you not love her?'

'Of course, we do. I am after all her mother. But I must think of the future.'

'What is the future? Surely it is your children?'

'That is what I mean. Kalindi's conduct has put her

family to shame. It is going to be a hurdle in finding a match for Usha. If we were to be seen as forgiving Kalindi for the step she took, we would be doubly shamed. Then the hurdle would be impossible to surmount.'

Esther turned to Usha and asked her gently, 'Is this what you want? That your parents should be so cruel towards your sister for the sake of your marriage?'

'My future is just an excuse. A sham. I know the real reason why they are pretending Kalindi does not exist,' Usha replied instantly.

Shantabai got angry. 'Are you saying that bringing Kalindi home will not affect your chances of marriage? Will it not bring your value in the marriage market down?'

'As though my value in that market is anything to talk about even now. I am coming round to what Kalindi and Aaba used to say—we should give up aspiring to be brahmins. We should simply accept our real caste. We are outcasts. No young man from among us, the outcasts, will devalue me because I live in the same house as Kalindi.'

Shantabai regarded her younger daughter with mounting anger. Esther did not want to be the cause of intensifying the conflict between mother and daughter. So she quickly changed the subject.

'Where is your brother these days?' she asked Usha.

'He was in Mumbai, but recently sent his things back home because he has decided to spend time travelling,' she replied.

'Travelling for work or pleasure?' Esther asked.

Shantabai said, 'For another reason altogether. You see, he is interested in the problem of caste. He was disappointed that Mumbai's Prarthana Samaj, which claims to oppose caste, does not act as if it does. He wants to find out whether the Arya Samaj and the Bramho Samaj are more sincere.'

Esther got the feeling that this was not the whole truth about Satyavrat. She put the subject aside for the moment, but soon went to Hujur Paga to meet Usha independently and probe for the truth. Usha was more than willing to give it to her. Satyavrat and his father had fallen out over Kalindi. Satyavrat had argued with his father saying Kalindi had done no wrong. 'Our caste was decided the day you married our mother. Your struggle to make brahmins accept her and your children into the caste was misguided. Kalindi experienced the reality of our situation and decided to live her life according to who we were in the eyes of society. If your marriage to Aai had failed to remove the stigma attached to her, evidently marriage did not have the power to change people's destinies. Then why marry at all? I think Kalindi's argument was pragmatic and therefore not wrong.'

Appasaheb was furious at his son's defence of Kalindi which, in the process, pointed an accusing finger at him. He said to Satyavrat, 'Your thinking is totally wrong. If this is what you really believe, I would request you to do what Kalindi did. Leave this house. I don't want your ideas to infect Usha.'

'Aha,' said Esther. 'So it is for your benefit that your parents have rejected their daughter *and* their son!'

Usha said, 'That is what they would like everybody, including themselves, to believe.'

16. Appasaheb Dagge

Appasaheb Dagge's habit was to look through the post when he returned from work, glance at the day's newspapers and go for a walk. Nobody ever came home to visit him. Nor did anybody accompany him on his walks. There was a time many years ago, when Shantabai would go with him. But when the children came, she had to stay home for them. Nor did she revert to the old habit after they had grown up and no longer required constant care.

Around the time Kalindi was eleven or twelve years old, he began to take her for a walk with him. At that age what could they talk about? They visited nobody and nobody visited them. Appasaheb's inter-caste marriage had made his family cut all relations with him. He was not a welcome member there and his wife's family were not welcome visitors in his home. As a result, there could be no small talk between father and daughter. Instead, their walks became an extension of school with Appasaheb taking Kalindi beyond school books into the wider world of knowledge. On one of these occasions when Kalindi had turned twelve, she asked him, 'Baba, you are a brahmin. Why didn't you marry a brahmin girl?'

Appasaheb was momentarily taken aback by the question. Had an adult asked him the same question, he might have spoken of social reform and moral courage—ideas which had become the pegs on which he had grown accustomed to hang his action. However, these were not ideas he could spout before his own daughter. To buy time he asked her, 'What makes you ask?'

Kalindi relpied, 'The girls in school don't drink water from my hands. They say your father might be brahmin but your mother isn't. So you are not brahmin.'

To this Appasaheb replied, 'That is the point, Kalindi. Most people believe in caste. I don't. That's why I married your mother.'

Soon after this conversation, Kalindi stopped accompanying him on his walks. She preferred to spend her evenings with her school friends.

Walking alone gave Appasaheb sufficient time to introspect and there was much in his life and actions to introspect about. Kalindi's leaving home had been an enormous shock to him. It was a time when he would have dearly loved to be able to discuss the problem and its consequences with his wife. But he could not, because that was when he became acutely aware of the mental distance between them. He realized that she was not interested in the social aspects of life. What she wanted and was happy with, was her security and comfort. These she had. The repercussions of Kalindi's act on their social position and on him personally did not interfere with them.

Looking back, he wondered why he had turned away the only marriage proposal he had received for Kalindi, which probably drove her to the irreversible action of leaving home and living with a married man as his mistress. Had he foreseen this, he would perhaps have given the proposal more thought. What made him reject it out of hand was his fear that if she married a man who was himself an outcast, he would have to give up forever the hope that his children would be accepted in society as brahmins. How could he have given up so easily on this hope? His marriage had been conducted with every legality and religious ritual in place. How then could his progeny be treated on par with children born out of wedlock? If the end for which he had struggled so hard was not to be attained, what kind of a father did it make him to have ruined a daughter's chances of a married life in pursuit of an impossible dream? Moral courage is a fine virtue to embrace if the end is achievable within one's lifetime. It appeared to him more and more impossible that Hindu society would ever rid itself of its caste divisions and discriminations. And yet he had rejected his daughter and driven away his son whose only crime was that he tried to make him understand the reason for which she had gone so tragically against social custom. How could he say Satyavrat was wrong? And if he was right, did it not behove him as a father to discuss with Kalindi why she had acted the way she did and treat her with sympathy? Now that his own actions had led not to securing his children's future but ruining it, why did he still dither to call himself an ass and a criminal of the first order? Was it only because his ego stood in the way?

Appasaheb was at a point in his introspection when

he felt acutely the need of guidance by someone who had thought deeply about caste, knew its roots, how deep they went and the chances of its ever being uprooted from Hindu society. He knew of only one man in Pune with whom he could discuss the questions raging in his mind. That person was Vaijanath Shastri. This historian had settled down in Deccan Gymkhana a few years ago and had been writing a great deal of late on sociological matters. He had once been Appasaheb's teacher but had been, in those days, a champion of the most regressive ideas which he would often articulate in class. He held that caste was not at all the discriminatory system that reformists declared it to be. On the contrary, caste assured equality. This equality functioned intra-caste. Within every caste every single person was equal. They did not see any reason to look beyond their caste for the most important things in life. You ate with your caste and married within your caste. For as long as you maintained your caste customs and practices, you did not need to concern yourself with what happened in other castes.

Reformists, he declared, wanted to break down the boundaries that mark each caste. What would they achieve if this were to happen? Was it really possible for the lower castes to feel happy marrying into the higher castes where they would always have to look for approval and acceptance? Man's sympathies were limited to small communities. Throw the door open to one and all and those who would normally look after their caste-brethren, particularly the poorer members of their caste, would end up not looking after anybody at all. 'Man has an unlimited capacity to wear himself out, to sacrifice his own happiness for those near and dear to him. Ask him to do the same in the name of universal brotherhood and you lose him. He does not see or know these brothers and sisters. Who then will he toil for?' he stated.

Students in those days were not prepared to accept what their teachers said merely because they had authority. They would ask Vaijanath Shastri awkward questions which they thought would make it difficult for him to defend his opinions. For instance, they pointed out that great thinkers like Justice Mahadev Ranade and Sir Devdatta Bhandarkar had opposed the caste system and that history had shown caste had been behind the ultimate collapse of the Maratha Empire. Vaijanath had an answer ready for both statements. 'What does that Mahadya Ranade know about history and that Dattya Bhandarkar about sociology?' he demanded. 'And if there was caste discrimination during Bajirao II's rule, did it not exist during Shivaji's rule when the empire was built? I take Mahadya and Dattya for a pair of bulls.'

When it got around that Vaijanath Shastri had been making these vituperative observations about the greats, he was asked to go. It was on account of this background that Appasaheb desisted for the time being from seeking Vaijanath Shastri's counsel on the questions that troubled him, although his current writings proved he thought somewhat differently now. Perhaps one day he would attend one of his lectures to feel the ground and only then approach him for a meeting.

17. Ramrao

Ramrao's office stood at the corner of Poybawadi. It was a two-room flat. The backroom served as his bedroom and a bachelor kitchen with a stove to make tea on, and a few pans and dishes. The furniture comprised a table and chair where he sat to have his lunch and dinner. A young boy called Sokya worked for him. His job was to wash Ramrao's clothes, have them pressed, fetch his lunch and dinner from the mess of which he was a member, wash his dishes and dust and sweep the two rooms.

Ramrao always wore a dhoti and was often bare-chested when he was in his private room. But when he entered the front room, his office, at eight o'clock in the morning, he came dressed impeccably in shirt and tie which he divested himself of only when his working hours were over late in the evening. His office was equipped with a desk at which he sat, a table for his typewriter, a cupboard for case files and one for books. Two benches were set against the wall across from his desk for his clients to sit on. The front door bore two nameplates side by side. One said, 'Ramrao Dhadphale, B.A. LLB. Advocate'. The other said, 'Rahatmag Union (Head Office and Parel Branch)'.

Naturally, the president of the Rahatmag Union was Ramrao Dhadphale and his clerk was the union secretary.

Ramrao had set up his office fairly recently. It had not existed when he met Kalindi on the train. He had been the secretary of another union then. The experience he gained there came in handy when he was thrown out. In those days people who devoted their lives to workers' welfare did so as social service. They were not professional unionists. They mouthed ideas like abolishing imperialism and capitalism because they wished to be taken for important contributors to national politics. Some workers' leaders were under the impression that they were funded by foreign powers who had a vested interest in the aims they championed. But this was not necessarily true. It was certainly not what drove them to talk about fighting imperialism. The real reason for that was their hope of being imprisoned for their work which would automatically give them credibility in the eyes of workers.

The question then remained of what these so-called union leaders survived on. The mystery was never solved. To say openly where their livelihood came from would be to diminish the nobility of their work. For then it would cease to be social service. It would become that ignoble thing, a job. This was one of the points of friction between them and Ramrao. He had proposed and continued to maintain that they should give themselves a fixed monthly salary of one hundred rupees. This suggestion caused the others to decide he was a rapacious, self-serving man who would only bring their work a bad name. It was then that the idea of discrediting him in order to cut off relations with him took root. The greatest crime that a union leader can be accused of is being secretly on the side of the mill-owners. To prove that Ramrao was a stooge, they made it generally known that he had once worked as a clerk in the office of the mill-owner Murar Deepchand. That was not all. He had also been a private tutor to his children. This was enough evidence of Ramrao's closeness to mill-owners. Worse still, Ramrao refused to claim that his work was to abolish imperialism and capitalism. He preferred the limited claim of ensuring that workers got just and fair treatment from their bosses.

Ramrao's childhood was spent in the Varhad region of Bombay Presidency but he grew up in Satar. His father, who had been in government service, had died when he was still a boy. However, he had been able to continue his schooling on his father's savings. He lost his mother when he was in his final year at school. He came to Mumbai for his college education, just about managing to eke out his father's savings till he graduated. When it came to studying law, he had to start earning his keep. That is when he found a job as a clerk in Murar Deepchand's office on a monthly salary of thirty rupees which was gradually increased to seventy-five. It was difficult for him to get his law degree in three years as students who did not have to earn their livelihood did. It took him five years to complete the course.

However, the protracted time he took to do it, along with the fact that he was working in a mill-owner's office all that time, gave him the opportunity to observe the lives of workers and mull over the lack of ethics in the mill-owners' business practices. There appeared to be no regulator to lay down ethical principles for businessmen. The sole principle that governed their work seemed to be 'might is right'. It was each man for himself and if you failed to protect your interests, nobody else would do it for you. Workers had no might so they could never be right. Without might, they had no way to protect their interests either. The only way they could get a fair deal was if somebody else led them. Ramrao discovered the levels of crookery mill-owners were willing to sink to in their greed for profits. He also discovered that the higher the social esteem they came to enjoy, the more the evil means they had employed to get there. They were quick to cut a worker's pay but the idea that the worker was their partner in business, the one who enabled them to earn their profits, never entered their heads. They found it perfectly possible to eat rich food and live in style while those who toiled at their machines starved and lived in dark, dingy tenements. This made Ramrao's blood boil.

At the end of those years of rumination, he came to a few conclusions. He saw that the government had very little interest in the welfare of workers. It was firmly on the side of mill-owners. It was not that they did not think they should show consideration for workers and their welfare. Of course, they should. However, if you were proposing steps to achieve this you had to speak in conciliatory tones and not be aggressive or too insistent in your demands. This is how things were to be done. The government is in favour of reforms; but the reforms must fall in line with their programmes. The way to draw attention to workers' plight then is for you to deliver a lecture on the subject. The government representative then follows up with his own much practised patter. You then show how happy you are with the government's response. The government also shows how happy it is with you. Not only have you given the government an opportunity to show how sympathetic they are to workers' welfare, but also to shed a few crocodile tears on their behalf. However, if you want to do real work, demand real rights for workers, the government soon shows you how unhappy that makes them. They decide you are a 'malcontent' bent on 'disturbing the peace' and charge you with 'sedition'. If you still choose to work hard and honestly for workers' welfare, you must be prepared to face two powerful enemies—the government and the mill-owner. To do this, you need to be fearless; and you also need to be single.

These are the conclusions that Ramrao's ruminations had led him to. The idea that he should remain single was not the end of this chain of thought alone. It was also the result of an earlier experience he had had. But that apart, he was convinced that you could not take on the responsibility of a wife if you were putting yourself at risk every day. When a woman married, she did so for peace and security. Therefore, no woman could possibly be a true helpmate to him in his work. He was not, by any means, a misogynist. His extremely respectful conduct towards women and the special trouble he took to fight for them when an injustice had been done was evidence enough of this. And let it be said that the women he fought for were not necessarily young and/or good-looking.

Given his thinking which went contrary to every prevalent idea, people who worked with him or observed his work had decided that he was a difficult man to understand.

18. Friendship Blossoms

After Ramrao rescued Kalindi from the advances of the 'teacher', it became her practice to visit his office after her morning's work for a chat. Ramrao soon realized that he was talking to a woman whom he did not know how to address. As far as he knew, she was Mrs Appa. That seemed rather a formal form of address for someone with whom he was becoming friendly. He remembered that her first name was Rose. He could address her as Rosebai but that sounded odd to his ears, combining as it did a very English name with a very Marathi suffix. However, that was her name and he had no choice but to call her by it. After he had addressed her as Rosebai on one or two occasions, she said, 'That's not my name.'

'Oh? What is your name then?'

'Kalindi.'

'So why did you tell us on the train that it was Rose?'

'It was a trick that a friend had suggested to me.'

'Why did you need a trick to tell us your name?'

'My friend said our people are extremely nosey. They will pester you with questions. Give yourself a name that is unfamiliar to them. That will set them off discussing it amongst themselves and relieve you of further questions.'

'That is true. They are indeed very nosey. But it is my experience that people are annoyed by their inquiries only if they have something to hide. I am not at all suggesting you are one of them; but surely you had a reason not to encourage their questions? Of course, I do know people who cannot stand being questioned by strangers.'

Kalindi, who had felt trapped by what Ramrao had said at first, was relieved when he said this which set her free. Still, she wished to give him a convincing reason for the trick she had used. So she said, 'You are right. I did in fact want to deflect needless questions because the people with whom I was going to stay here were Bene Israel, the community to which my friend belongs. If I had told the passengers where I was going to stay, I would have been asked why with Bene Israels. There is a long story behind that which I didn't want to tell total strangers.'

'Not a bad trick to put people off questioning. I must try it some time. So your real name is Kalindi?'

'That's right.'

'In that case is Appa really your surname?'

'No, it isn't. I'm Kalindi Dagge.'

'Mrs Kalindi Dagge?'

'No, Miss.'

'So, you are single then?'

'I am.'

'Why don't you wear kumkum?'

'I don't much care for it. But more than that, since I've been staying with Bene Israels, and they don't wear kumkum, I do likewise. As they say, do in Rome as Romans do.'

The conversation had been a revelation for Ramrao. This young woman whom he had taken to be Mrs Appa, a Telugu, had turned out to be a Marathi woman of rare spirit. One who was broadminded enough to be staying with Bene Israels, who was educated enough to have found herself a job in Mumbai, who was earning enough to be able to stand on her own feet and who, to top it all, had deep sympathy for the very people for whose welfare he was working. This could be the foundation for a welcome friendship. Ramrao began to look forward eagerly to her visits although he thought they were mistimed. They came in the middle of his busiest schedule, making it impossible for him to relax and chat. Soon he felt there was enough understanding between them to suggest that, instead of her coming to his office, he would come by to her place in the evenings after work when they could go out, see the sights of Mumbai and exchange the day's news. Kalindi had no reason to turn down his suggestion. Had she been living in a Hindu household, she would have been forced to do so. Her landlady, whoever she might have been, would surely have behaved like a domineering mother-in-law, keeping an eagle eye on Kalindi's movements. Mrs Sarah Ashtamkar and her daughters, on the other hand, thought nothing of it except as an excuse to tease her. Kalindi enjoyed their jokes. It tickled her that they pretended she was to marry Ramrao soon.

When Kalindi and Ramrao went out on their walks, their conversation was often about what they saw. But more than that, they spoke about the workers' living conditions. Ramrao took special pleasure in talking about the workers' movement, partly because he wanted to share his knowledge of the subject with her, but more importantly because he, being a leader of the movement, automatically came into the picture. To boast about one's work showed a lack of civility; but it could not be denied that if people, particularly a young woman, heard about it incidentally and was impressed, it doubled the delight of sharing knowledge. It goes without saying that he only talked about his work because Kalindi showed great interest in it. She did not merely show interest. She genuinely felt it. So he told her about the time the workers of a certain mill struck work and his negotiations with the managers produced a solution. He told her about how his growing weight with workers made the leaders of other unions envious and how they spread canards about him to bring him into disrepute. He told her that, if his weight with the workers had grown, it was because they saw he was genuinely concerned for their well-being. He did not encourage them to go on strike at the drop of a hat, which would lead them into worse penury. Expressing admiration for this, Kalindi said, 'That's absolutely the right policy if workers' welfare is the aim. The women I interview give me vivid descriptions of what happens when their men go on strike and stay home for a week or two. The expenses on food increase. It isn't just food, but constant cups of tea and bidis. Their tea cans are empty at the end of two days and the women have no money for milk. But men continue to smoke their bidis, buying them on credit when their money runs out. The bidi shops stop giving credit after a while. With neither tea to drink nor bidis to smoke, the men start to fret and become aggressive. They start beating their wives and children. There have been instances of women walking out on their husbands when they can no longer take the beatings. By the time the strike is called off, debts have mounted to such a level that it takes them a year or more to pay them off.'

'Your experiences are teaching me about a side of workers' lives that I know nothing of. This knowledge will help me immensely in my work. So which areas does your field work cover?'

'Mainly between Dadar and Tardeo. But the centre of my research is in Parel. When I enter these neighbourhoods, I feel I'm in some alien world. Here people work with their hands and both men and women do the same work. Hierarchies depend on who makes more money. I have observed that, if a son makes more than a father, he begins to call the shots in the house. Money is definitely king. In this kingdom women have full citizen rights unlike women of our class.'

'What a shame that you feel the need to use words that belong to monarchies. That is not what we want the workers' world to be. We want it to be an industrial democracy.'

'At the moment I can't say it is. More like an anarchy where money is might and might is money.'

'Surely it isn't as bad as that?'

'Probably not. I exaggerate. But I've heard of a woman supervisor, who decides on the fortunes of the women who work under her. She takes bribes and gives bribes. She also employs good-looking young women for the managers' pleasure. Everybody knows about her activities. They talk behind her back about them. But when they come face to face with her, they can't stop flattering her, because that's the side their bread is buttered on.'

'We must fight against these practices. Only then will we achieve our goal of an industrial democracy.'

'Whom do you mean by„ we„?' Kalindi asked pointedly.

Ramrao smiled and said, 'I and whosoever believes in the same ideas as me and is willing to work towards the goal I've set for myself.'

19. Kalindi Visits Pune

Kalindi was on one of her visits to Pune. She went as often as she could to be with Chintamani. As days went by, she began to feel that the bond he had with Esther's mother had grown much stronger than the bond he had shared with her. It was a bitter-sweet discovery. Sweet because it made her feel less guilty about abandoning him. Bitter because it made her feel abandoned. She blamed Shivsharanappa bitterly for the separation he had brought upon mother and son, little knowing that it was the demands of his life with her that had brought him to a point where he could no longer look after her and their son.

This time Esther had news to give her regarding Shivsharanappa's present condition. That night, as the friends prepared to go to bed, Esther said, 'I have seen your Shivsharanappa.'

Kalindi sat up, instantly tense. 'Not my Shivsharanappa, please. Where did you see him?'

'At the racecourse.'

'Esther? What were you doing there?'

'I was there with a relative who had a ticket to spare.'

'You mean he gambled? You gambled?'

'Of course not. Although being there made me realize what tempted people to gamble.'

'What?'

'It's such a thrill to see those magnificent horses run, trying to outrace each other, the jockeys bent over them urging them to go faster, the spectators crying themselves hoarse. I found myself yelling with them for a horse that was lagging behind.'

'Always on the side of the underdog.'

'Of course. And he did speed up.'

'Because of you?'

'I didn't say that. But we are talking about Shivsharanappa, not horses.'

'Yes, of course. How did you run into him? The racecourse is huge.'

'He was in the same stand as us.'

'And how did you recognize him?'

'One of the men sitting near us pointed him out to the other as Appasaheb Dagge's son-in-law.'

'Oh! He actually dignified him with that name?'

'He did. But the other caught him out. You mean the fellow who kidnapped Appasaheb Dagge's daughter and kept her?'

'Kind of him to think I didn't run away to him of my own accord. Perhaps because that would reflect on my parents and the values they had inculcated in me.'

'You are still bitter.'

'Of course, I am. It's been three years since I left Pune. But Pune still talks about me.'

'Pune has nothing else to do. But I think what I gathered about Shivsharan from those two men might upset you.'

'What?'

'That he gambles and drinks. He has won large amounts betting on horses who are not necessarily the best runners.'

'Meaning?'

'There's a racket going on. You can bribe jockeys to fix races. He throws parties for them.'

'If there's a racket, aren't there other punters who profit by it?'

'There must be.'

'That means those who don't have money to bribe, lose whatever money they have. And those who have money get more.'

'Yes. That's about it.'

'And Shivsharan is involved.'

'Apparently he made huge losses in his business and this was the only way he knew of getting rich quick.'

'So why should this news upset me? He's getting rich.'

'But also drinking. And gambling doesn't always pay. One day he'll sink and be ruined.'

'I suppose we all have to pay for our choices and mistakes. He made me pay for mine.'

'You have become very hard-hearted towards him. I had thought I could persuade you to meet him and tell him to give up gambling and drinking if only for your son's sake.'

'Why should I? I am perfectly capable of looking after my son.'

'Kalindi, you were once in love with this man. You lived together like husband and wife. He is your son's father. Don't you have a shred of feeling left for him?'

Kalindi thought for a while. Then said, 'Actually no. I don't think I want to even see his face.'

'Well,' Esther sighed. 'Perhaps that is what people mean when they say the wife's love for her husband is stronger than a mistress's love for her man. A wife will keep coaxing her husband to give up his ruinous ways so that their life together is restored to what it was.'

'Of course, she would. Because she is bound to him for life. What he does with his life affects her directly. The mistress is the first to be thrown out when the man hits rock bottom. She is expendable. The wife isn't. He too is tied to her for life. What you call love is just that. Social compulsion.'

Esther thought about what Kalindi had said and had to agree. 'Well, I'm glad you're not upset. Time to give you another bit of news I managed to dig out.'

She told Kalindi of her visit to her parents' home and her meeting with Usha later where she discovered that Satyavrat had not betrayed her as Kalindi thought he had. 'He wasn't given your letter. He was in Mumbai then.' Esther told Kalindi about the disagreement he had had with their father over her conduct, her father's anger and his ultimatum—if that's how you feel, leave this house.

'And this happened while I was living in that dingy room in Shukravar Peth, eking out a living and cursing the fact that even Satyavrat had abandoned me. I was on the point of ending my life when I met you, Esther. Why could he not have told me, written to me?'

'You forget that your letter was not given to him so he had no idea where you were or what had happened to you. Why does it upset you so much now? You've done well for yourself.'

'Now, yes. But instead of living through that hell in Shukravar, I could have gone to Mumbai and stayed with him. We could have discussed our plans.'

'What plans?'

'Of starting a caste exclusively for those marginalized by so-called respectable society. Half-breeds like us who belong to neither this caste nor that.'

'Did you intend including people like us? Bene Israels, Christians, Parsis?'

'Those who were discards from their communities like we were, surely.'

'The time isn't lost yet,' Esther said, ending their conversation. 'I have his address for you.'

20. Satyavrat's Letter

Travelling around north Hindustan, Satyavrat had made Delhi his headquarters. He spent several months there just looking around, absorbing a city that had been the capital of the country chiefly because Hindustan's invaders, its enemies, had made it their seat. Later, he travelled all over Punjab and neighbouring regions. One day he found himself waiting for a train at the Meerut Cantonment station when he heard that there was a trial going on against Communist revolutionaries. His curiosity aroused, he attended some hearings and came away filled with several questions. So, these people thought private property was at the bottom of all inequalities, including caste. Once private property was abolished, all disparities would vanish and equality would reign. Sitting in the waiting room of the station, Satyavrat tried to imagine a society without private property. However hard he tried, he simply could not imagine such a society.

However, he had made some progress in his study of the Arya Samaj and found that they were closer to being casteless than the Prarthana Samaj. They were not given to making grand statements about the world as one family, the way Brahmo Samajists were. Their attention was concentrated more on the ground on which they stood, where they found an abundance of inequality which needed correcting. Satyavrat found that they had greater compassion for the downtrodden. Comparing what he saw amongst them with what he had experienced in his society in Pune, the chief difference he found was that the Arya Samaj did not use labels like widow and half-breed and bastard to ostracize people. Whatever people's marital status, whatever their caste, they were all afforded the same prestige as any others in society. Satyavrat began to wonder if he should join the Arya Samaj where he would not be treated with contempt. But that would only solve his personal problem. Maharashtra would still remain a society full of caste discrimination, exclusion, contempt and ostracism. How was that to be changed? Who could he discuss this problem with? He looked back to the times when he could always discuss these issues with Kalindi. He wished he could, even now. Perhaps he could. Perhaps he only needed to get back in touch with her and discover how she felt and thought these days.

He instantly uncapped his fountain pen and wrote her a letter. Although he addressed it to Kalindi, he would send it to Usha with a request to hand it over to Kalindi. Here is what the letter said:

The Waiting Room
Meerut Cantonment Station

Dear Tai,

I have no idea what your state of mind is these days. I heard from Aai that you have a son whom you have named Chintu. Why Chintu? I can't understand that.

Our mother's father was called Chintopant. Surely you don't hold his memory so sacred as to name your son after him! Or is Chintu a short form of Chintamani, the wish-fulfilling gem?

I had really wanted to come and see you when you had Chintu; but I wondered how Shivsharanappa would take my coming. Surely he would not like it. But soon I admitted to myself that it was not his liking or not liking my coming that was the problem. It was I who did not want to set eyes on him. I absolve you of all guilt over what you did; but I cannot forgive him. I cannot forgive the bastard for having led my sister down the wrong path.

But let me not dwell on him. Thinking about you, I feel certain that you are leading a happy life with Shivsharanappa and your son. You must be spending all your time playing with Chintu, indulging him, cooking him his favourite food. But meanwhile we remain in exactly the same situation in our society as we have always been. I doubt if you have either the inclination or the time to think about the larger question regarding a casteless society that we used to discuss so animatedly years ago. On the personal level, I have given much thought to what you have always said about our father's action in marrying our mother. According to you he did it entirely for social praise, to establish himself in the eyes of society as a progressive man while not caring a whit about how his action would affect us, his children. I am now convinced that the nobility of motive that drove him to do what he did, cannot be besmirched because of the results—totally unexpected to him—it produced. The work that Baba was undertaking through his personal action was much too large for it to be completed in his lifetime. But that doesn't mean his aim was not worth striving for with the hope that, at some time in the future, it would be achieved. It might take two or more generations for this to happen. But I cannot believe it never will.

I see your action as a continuation of Baba's. He was pushing ahead with not a single glance backwards. Your action amounted to saying, whether you achieve your aim or not depends wholly on how open and evolved our society is. We knew it wasn't. He knew it wasn't. And so we became victims. Your action was to accept our mother's past and re-establish a link with it through the decision you made. If, despite her background, or because of it, Baba had married her, and in so doing, hoped to return to her the social prestige that had been denied to her, you did what you did to demand social prestige for yourself. Baba could not see this vital link between his action and yours. If he had really respected Aai as a human being rather than a member of a class or caste, he would not have rejected you as he did. There he fell short of my expectations.

The question facing us on the bigger social level remains the same. How are people to be respected despite their personal choices of whom they marry or despite the presence in them of mixed blood or despite what their parentage is or isn't. We need to build a strong social movement to achieve these aims. But meanwhile, I do believe that the Arya Samaj is at least halfway there. Our own Prarthana Samaj, that poor, moribund body, is hardly capable of even aiming at the widespread changes in social attitudes and beliefs that are called for if we are to achieve what we are talking about. This task demands men of independent spirit, commitment and industry. Where are they to be found in Maharashtra? Prarthana Samaj is led by men who have spent entire lifetimes polishing British boots and finding their greatest reward in doing so. A man who stands up and says to society, the way forward is to abolish caste and become all-inclusive, to judge people by the work they do and not by what their parents did, has to be a human being of outstanding intellect and charisma. Moreover, he needs to be seen practising what he preaches if his listeners, who have lived in a certain way for centuries and whose way of life comes from deep religious beliefs, are to pay him any heed at all. Our father is not such a man, nor are those who lead Prarthana Samaj. However, I do believe that the Arya Samaj cares about society and its individuals. I have been attending their lectures here and feel more and more certain that I should join the organization. I am not in agreement with some of their ideas, but the most important thing for me is that the organization was founded by a man of independent spirit and thinking. Prarthana Samaj, on the other hand, was founded by people who had enjoyed the patronage of the British. Their protection was never extended to people like Baba and us, his progeny. We had to live with the label of that shameful thing, half-breeds. We must fight against the stigma ourselves. The Arya Samaj didn't gain entry into Maharashtra. Outsiders claim that we are particularly impervious to movements led by people who don't belong to our parts. This is not only true but it is a situation regarding which the people of Maharashtra feel gratified. We have two choices before us. Either we join the Arya Samaj and find our rightful place in society or, as you used to say, we create a society comprising all those who have been cast out by society for one reason or another and build a powerful force of well-educated, prestigious people.

But perhaps you are no longer in a frame of mind to take an interest in these social questions. You are, in a way, settled in life. You are probably too involved in bringing up your children and ensuring a good future for them. Usha is now an adult. She will benefit by reading this letter. She too must start thinking of the problem she will soon face regarding our position in society.

My travels in the north have proved profitable. I have made good money. Although the Arya Samaj dismisses the Mahabharata along with the Puranas, it sells. It allows me to make a living. In the six months that I have spent in these parts, I have sold four hundred copies. I get a commission of eight annas per copy. So I have made over three thousand rupees. After deducting expenditure on lodging and boarding, I am left with net savings of two thousand rupees. Now if I decide to study Law, I will not have to ask Baba to support me.

There are good dharmashalas in the north. The eateries are not so good. One chapati costs one paisa and puri-bhaji is available everywhere. In the dharmashala, you get a special room for four annas extra per day. In Delhi you have hotels like Sardar Griha and there is a club for people from the south. Things are comfortable. I cannot say I am unhappy.

I look forward to a reply from you.

Your brother,

Aaba

Satyavrat posted this letter in the red mail box at Meerut Cantonment station. When the khansama came to take his 'arder', he asked for one curry-rice and a side dish, then returned to his newspapers.

21. Kalindi's Advice to Ramrao

Kalindi was back in Mumbai on Monday as had been her routine since she started her job. After she had made her rounds, collected her facts and figures, she went to Ramrao's office where she found him making jottings on a sheet of paper.

'What are all those figures? A new kind of mathematics?' she asked.

'Just a poor attempt at cracking a very big problem,' he answered, pushing his papers away and looking up at her with a smile.

'Problem?'

'Call it a dream.'

'Won't you share it with me?'

'To rid workers of their abject poverty.'

'That dream will never come true. There will always be the very rich and the very poor.'

'That is how it is. That is how it has been. But it doesn't need to be that way forever.'

'That's not just a dream. It's a fantasy.'

'Every ideal is a fantasy until it is realized.'

'Perhaps you are right. But speaking for myself, I'm very wary of people who run after ideals.'

'Why is that?'

'That's because they chase dreams that might come true centuries later but meanwhile they destroy the lives of their wives and children.'

'Kalindi, I think you are speaking from experience. You aren't parroting what you were taught at school. Weren't you taught to believe that every human being must have ideals and must live for them? Anyway, idealists don't bite, you know.'

'They don't bite the world. But they do bite their families.'

'I demand an explanation for that view. How are we a problem for our wives and children?'

'This is how. Ideals call for self-sacrifice. Idealists make the sacrifices that are called for without hesitation. But have their wives and children signed up for the sacrifice? Are they even asked? They are simply dragged along to end up with nothing. Idealists at least earn praise if nothing else. I don't call that self-sacrifice. I call it family-sacrifice.'

'Do you deny idealists the right to live in the world?'

'I only deny them the right to marry and produce children.'

'You are absolutely right there. It is a thought that has been uppermost in my mind for years. It began with trying to decide whether I should marry. But it could include others like me. You have just resolved the last shred of doubt in my mind. I now know I must not marry. But with that resolve, another tricky question, which has to do with my colleagues in the movement, crops up. I have never known how to judge the lifestyle they have adopted.'

'What lifestyle is that?'

'Let me explain. See, as labour leaders, we have no means of livelihood. We can't live off the very people we are trying to save from exploitation. Some of us make money by cooking the books a bit. But by and large, we are penurious. This puts marriage out of the question for us. And so...'

'And so?'

'I don't know how to put this to a chaste woman like you.'

For a moment Kalindi savoured the bitter irony of being referred to as a chaste woman before returning to her questioning.

'Look, you can't arouse my curiosity and then refuse to feed it.'

'I will answer, but on one condition. I don't want to be blamed if what I say offends your delicate sensibilities.'

'Ramrao, you are speaking to a woman who has been roaming the labour areas and has seen the most brutal truths about human life. So please don't hold back on account of my delicate sensibilities.'

'In that case, this is the situation as it stands among my colleagues. If we are going to spend our lives fighting for our principles, we will not marry.'

'That's a decision taken by centuries of idealists who have fought for principles or their country.'

'Yes, but we are not as naïve as to believe that living without marriage means living without women. We need women as much as anybody else. Some of us have found a solution to the problem in following the Pandava dharma.'

'Meaning?'

'See, there are women leaders amongst us who are themselves married but are free to co-habit with others. Since communists don't believe in marriage, they have no problem with co-habiting without marriage.'

'But how do these women fit into communist principles? Surely, they should also not marry? If they give in to convention then they must abide by its rules. You can't have it both ways.'

'I suppose you are right. But that's a problem for the women to sort out. As far as we are concerned, we are doing no wrong by sleeping with the same woman.'

'So now that you have arrived at a decision not to marry, will you too become a follower of the Pandava dharma?' A tremor entered Kalindi's voice as she asked the question.

'I am not speaking about myself. But as a general rule, I would say idealists have no choice but to adopt that lifestyle.'

'To my mind there is another alternative.'

'Which is?'

'Marry a woman who is financially independent. An idealist will not have to support her then. She will support him.'

'But why would a woman who is earning a good salary want to marry a poor idealist?'

'Because just as a man needs a woman, a woman needs a man.'

'Yes, but our world is full of people who are only too ready to point fingers at women who„ marry below them„.

Earning women would be inhibited in their choice because of what such people might say.'

'I'm fully aware of those stupid calculations. A woman who has a graduate degree must marry a post-graduate at the least. A woman who is this tall must marry a man who is that tall. I have no patience for these idiotic rules. I would love to tear that rule book into shreds. So please give my message of a third alternative to your colleagues. I know the minds of women who are over thirty, single and financially independent. They will marry men who have no income but are doing good work and want to marry.'

'Even suppose such women exist, a man may not want to propose marriage for fear of being rejected.'

'Is it so hard to accept rejection? Don't both women and men face several rejections in the marriage market? Does that hurt so much?'

'It doesn't. My doubts go back to your original assertion that women of the kind you describe would be willing to marry a man with no fixed income. You speak confidently of women you know. But I know women of another kind.'

'What kind?'

'Women who don't look at their jobs as lifelong commitments but stopgaps. They are on the lookout for husbands who earn well enough to support them. As soon as such a husband is found, they happily hop out of a full-time job into a full-time marriage.'

'Perhaps you're right.'

'I know of a nurse who married a man to escape her need to work. She was looking to him to support her. But he had other ideas. He was looking forward to living off her. Marriage revealed the differences in their expectations. They are still married but have bitter fights every day.'

'That is a sad story. But on the plus side, you communists have a wider choice than other men. You have no problems with a woman's caste or with her being a widow. On their part, widows and lower-caste women have almost given up hope of marriage. So they would be more open to proposals from you labour leaders. Do tell your colleagues that.'

Ramrao gave Kalindi a broad smile. 'I'll do that,' he said. 'But right now, I am expecting a few people for a meeting. So can we quickly finish off our work? What are today's figures?'

Later Ramrao found himself wondering what Kalindi's advice to him had meant. Was she suggesting that she would not take it amiss if he were to propose to her?

22. Appasaheb Looks Back

Satyavrat, not knowing Kalindi's address, had sent his letter to Usha. He was under the impression that Kalindi was still with Shivsharanappa. The envelope contained two letters, one for Kalindi and the other for Usha herself. In his letter to Usha, he had requested her to hand over his letter to Kalindi without Shivsharanappa's knowledge. He had also requested her to show both letters to Appasaheb first. This request would have put Usha in a quandary, given the fact that their father had prohibited them from communicating with Kalindi after she left the house. He would then have suspected that Satyavrat had been communicating with Kalindi through her and she would have had to bear the brunt of his bitter displeasure.

As it happened, she did not have to face such a situation directly because her father had made it a practice, ever since Kalindi had left home, to open and read every letter that came addressed to Usha. It happened in this case too. He had already read both of Satyavrat's letters before handing them to her. Usha waited for the expected explosion, but it did not come. Appasaheb's only reaction to the letters was to say to Usha, 'When you write to Aaba, please tell him that he has not made his thoughts regarding future action in the caste issue very clear in his letter. Tell him I would like him to come home so that we can discuss the issue face to face.'

Usha and Shantabai were both taken by surprise by the implications of what Appasaheb had said. The first was that he did not mind the family reopening communication with Kalindi. The second was that Satyavrat had been forgiven and invited home. Usha rejoiced at this turn of events and rushed to meet Esther with the news the following day. She gave her Satyavrat's letter to Kalindi to be sent on to Mumbai and also informed her that she would write to Satyavrat immediately, urging him to come home as soon as possible.

Satyavrat's letter had given Appasaheb two reasons to be happy. The first and obvious one was that his son would soon return home. The second was his realization that Satyavrat had given deep and careful thought to a problem that had exercised his own mind for a long time. The letter brought home to him a truth that he had been somewhat blinded to. He had fought against society as an individual, but he had not looked at his fight as only the beginning of a battle. Although Satyavrat and Kalindi's position in society, which had made life difficult for them, was the starting point of Satyavrat's reflections on the issue, he had gone beyond the personal to contemplate the larger question involved. He had been busy looking around at organizations which appeared to be fighting the same fight with varying degrees of success. His was a clear-eyed look at the ground reality unlike Appasaheb's view, clouded as it had been by a false belief in his own idealism. He became acutely aware that he had never had an open discussion with his children about the issues that were going to affect their lives directly. Of course, there was a reason for not doing so. He did not want to hear his children criticize him for marrying a woman of a lower caste and plunging their future into darkness. Kalindi had not waited for him to discuss the problem with them. She had spoken her mind with brutal honesty when she walked out of the house. He was too angry then, his ego too deeply hurt for him to put himself in her place and see the situation from her point of view. His stubbornness had finally forced his son also to leave the house.

Appasaheb had felt then that his whole life had come crashing down around his ears. His anger and ego had made him a lonely man. He tried sharing his anxieties and thoughts with his wife. She, however, had no interest in discussing his ideas. She regarded them not as possible plans for the future but as dreams that he amused himself with, just as a poor man builds castles in the air about making money and becoming rich. His wife had no time for idealism. She had no complaints against life. She had never given up anything to achieve a goal based on a principle or a value. Her great satisfaction lay in the fact that she, the daughter of a kept woman, had become the legally wedded wife of a brahmin. If this had not produced the hoped-for result of her being accepted into the community, her answer had been to join the Brahmos, whom Appasaheb viewed as unconscionable fakes. So sold was she on them that she had tried to persuade him to discard his sacred thread. There had been a heated argument between them when he had decided to celebrate Satyavrat's thread ceremony.

He had now begun to question his own motives in clinging to his caste. He wondered what Satyavrat's thoughts about this might be. Satyavrat belonged to the next generation. Satyavrat might be able to prove to him that thinking as a brahmin was not the best way to solve the social problem that faced them. It was these and other similar thoughts that had lain behind his request to Satyavrat to return home.

Esther, on her part, had forwarded Satyavrat's letter to Kalindi. Both she and Usha now looked forward to Satyavrat's return to Pune and a positive development in Appasaheb's relationship with his children.

23. Vaijanath Shastri: The First Dose

When Appasaheb visited Vaijanath Shastri, he was living in a tiny bungalow in the Deccan Gymkhana neighbourhood. His wife Shardabai had died and he had been forced, once again, to endure widowerhood. Having to fend for himself, his studies in grammar and comparative linguistics were often interrupted. When Appasaheb had decided to ask Vaijanath Shastri for a meeting, he had wondered how he was to tell him about his life, his decisions, his disappointment in their outcome—in short, his entire sordid sob story. However, when the time came, he discovered that Vaijanath already knew every single detail about his life, including the sub-plot of Kalindi's abandonment of home and her decision to live with a married man. His letter had only said, 'It seems to me that any man working towards the abolition of caste discrimination in Hindustan today, lands himself in deep trouble. I would dearly like to know your thoughts on the matter for which reason I seek a meeting when I could engage in a discussion with you about the problem. If you agree to see me, could you inform me of a suitable day and time when I could visit you?' Appasaheb included a few memories of school in the letter to further his cause.

Vaijanath Shastri responded in the affirmative to Appasaheb's request for a meeting, adding, 'My time at home is spent writing. I believe the only reason to sit under a roof is if you want to write. There is no justification for it if we do not want to write but talk. Therefore, I would rather not grant you a meeting in my house. Instead, I would be happy if you accompanied me on my walk. I intend on walking to Pagdya Maruti hill on Sunday at three o'clock in the afternoon. I would welcome your company then. In your letter you recall an incident that happened when you were my student. You had thrown a pebble at a water pot that a woman was carrying on her head and broken it. You recall me fining you four annas and ordering you to pay the money to the woman. But I recall something more. I made you stand on your bench for three hours. I remember the entire incident very well. It is on that account that I have been following your progress since. I am in possession of every single detail about your life and would welcome a meeting with you.'

Appasaheb met and accompanied Vaijanath Shastri on his walk to Pagdya Maruti hill the following Sunday. As they passed by Deccan Gymkhana, Vaijanath launched into a diatribe. 'This place has become a breeding ground for mosquitoes. The first people to commit the sin of choosing it for their establishment were the founders of Fergusson College. Who knows how many victims malaria will claim because of that original sin. People who come to settle here have no idea how soon it is going to turn into a desolate wasteland. I have been bitten sore by mosquitoes ever since I came. Deccan Gymkhana will soon be another old Goa. Our people have shown as little sense as the Portuguese in the sixteenth century.'

The pair now turned into Bhandarkar Institute Road. Here Vaijanath held forth on how big a part Kurtakoti had played in the building of the memorial to Bhandarkar and the role Bhandarkar had played in raising Kurtakoti to the level of Shankaracharya. Appasaheb heard him out in silence, without adding any critical comments of his own to this flow of observations. He was himself not too keen to start discussing the questions on his mind until they had reached a quieter spot. Soon they were climbing the hill behind Bhandarkar Institute. Halfway up, Vaijanath Shastri stopped, looked around and asked, 'So what question is bothering you?'

Appasaheb answered, 'Must people fighting against caste discrimination resign themselves to social debasement, which seems to me the inevitable consequence?'

'That depends on what their objective is. Those who only talk about it do more harm than good. If they want to do good, they must have a concrete programme in hand. They wish to break down the caste system. Fine. But what do they want to put in its place? They must have a grander plan than just fighting. Perhaps they should create a single caste that is superior to all existing castes and will replace them.'

'How is that to be done? What kind of caste would that be?'

'The man who knows the answer to that would have to be a supreme human being.'

'So, you don't know?'

'I only have a few vague ideas at this moment. But they will soon acquire a more definite form.'

'Can you at least tell me whether you think trying to break the caste system is wrong in principle?'

'Not at all. But who is trying to break the caste system and for what reason is the root question.'

'In that case, is it possible today for the fight against caste to succeed?'

'There have been attempts in every age to break the caste system and the route has always been to create a new caste. Do you want to create yet another caste?'

'I want to go further. I want to create a caste that will enjoy social prestige.'

'The individual who aims at such a thing needs to have a great deal of determination. You are not that person.'

'Are you doubting the strength of my mind?'

'Indeed I am.'

'And why is that?'

'You rejected your daughter outright. Why?'

'What else could I have done when she brought a bad name to the entire community of educated women? Praise her for her act?'

'What did she do that was so wrong that it led to the result you describe?'

'Don't you think she did wrong?'

'No, I don't.'

'What?'

'What she did was claim her right to cohabit with a man of her choice and become a mother of his child without submitting to his absolute power.'

'Is it right for women to want motherhood outside marriage?'

'Why is it wrong? All they are doing is contravening prevalent social customs.'

'But isn't that wrong?'

'I don't think so. These so-called social customs that women are supposed to live by, have been made by middle- and upper-class men on whom women and children are dependent. Women live under their obligation forever because they are fed, clothed and housed by them. But this population of women is just a fraction of the whole. Society has never given a thought to the rules and customs that should govern financially independent women. It is time they did that. Did you, for example, ask your daughter why she did what she did?'

'No.'

'Which means you condemned her without giving her a chance to speak on her own behalf.'

'What are you getting at?'

'If your aim is to create a new caste, you will have to think of a new morality and a new social goal. You have not understood the social structure on which your action and hers are based. Your mother-in-law was a teacher, a self-supporting woman. She rejected the idea of a husband and bore a child out of wedlock. You tell yourself that what she did was wrong and that you showed great generosity in marrying her daughter. You also think that your daughter did wrong in living with a man who was not her husband. Every single one of these ideas is the sign of a conservative mind. Neither your mother-in-law nor daughter has done wrong. The problem is that you haven't understood the secrets of their lives.'

'I suppose you have understood them?'

'Yes.'

'What have you understood?'

'Your mother-in-law had made a matriarchal family for herself. Yet she allowed her daughter to withdraw from it and enter a patriarchal family instead. Your daughter, in her turn, recognized her legacy and built a matriarchal family.'

'Oh no. Not her. She was not self-supporting like her grandmother. These are all theoretical concepts. What they suggest is that a courtesan is not a fallen woman but a woman who has adopted the matriarchal social system.'

'You are dead right. A courtesan is not a fallen woman. When women begin to earn their own keep, none of the restrictions imposed on them by men will endure. A new system must be created for these women. Women who sing and dance are said to be unchaste. However, in matters of feelings and personal aspirations, they are no different from their brahmin sisters.'

'That may be true. But the similarity ends with hearts and emotions. Where the mind is concerned, education and culture make all the difference between them and upper-caste women.'

'Don't talk to me about education. The only thing that makes a difference is the financial dependence on men of upper-class women. Not burdened with the responsibility of earning their keep is what naturally makes their lives, choices, actions different from women who earn their keep.'

'If financial independence is going to lead women to this, I would say they should not have it.'

'But that is not going to happen howsoever much you might wish it. Single women and widows will have to earn their living. Wives of feeble, incapacitated husbands would also have to carry the burden of supporting them. Even women who do not have to, will increasingly seek financial independence. Nothing will stop them now. So you might as well face reality and change your moral rules to suit women who earn their keep.'

'And what would those rules be?'

At that point Vaijanath Shastri realized talking while walking had knocked the breath out of him. So he lowered himself on a rock, lit a bidi, took a couple of drags and then turned to Appasaheb's question.

'To begin with, any woman who is about to enter the marital state must be given the freedom to choose whether she wishes to live in a patriarchal or a matriarchal family. If she chooses the matriarchal system, she automatically gets the right to throw her husband out of the house if she so wishes. Naturally, she has no rights to her husband's property and the husband has no rights over their children.'

'Absolutely nobody will accept your reforms, not Hindus who have been raised to live by what our ancient sages have taught, nor indeed today's progressives.'

'So be it. But there will still be some who agree with me. They will find my ideas acceptable.'

'So you consider yourself above all our great religious teachers, do you?'

'Yes. I know more history than what was available to them in their times. So do not throw their greatness at me.'

'Sages like Vasisth and Vishwamitra...'

'I, Vaijnath, am greater than any of them.'

Appasaheb was silenced for a while. Then he said, 'Are all the ideas you have spoken of today yours?'

'Well, I will admit that their primary source was my wife's friend Priyamvada Godbole. She used to say that all religious rules have been made by men who belong to the class that provides for its women. Why should they be imposed on all other women? Seventy-five per cent of the women in this country work to earn bread for their families. To inflict on them rules meant for the remaining twenty-five per cent is sheer injustice. She used to insist that women made the nation. They were the nation, not men. If the greater part of the male populace were to die, women would still ensure the continuance of future generations of human beings using the men that remained. If all the women died and every man that was born, lived, the nation would soon die for lack of citizens. For this reason, men cannot be given the right to decide the ethics of reproduction. This is what my wife's friend told her repeatedly.'

'So, according to you, what constitutes sin and what brings religious merit?'

'Ideas of sin and virtue change with time in every religion. True followers of Vedanta do not believe in either. If that is so, should ideas of morality not be reviewed from time to time? Brahmins who have created the rules in the first place are the only ones who have the power to change or overturn them. Therefore, I, Vaijanath Shastri, hereby declare the following: a woman who bears a child out of wedlock is not automatically a sinner. Unwed motherhood has been condemned because a woman who lives with a man out of wedlock does not have rights over the man's property. Nor do their progeny. So the basis for this morality is money. It has nothing to do with spirituality or divine decree. If women who bear children out of wedlock and the children themselves are routinely condemned to penury today, what need is there for further social condemnation?'

'You think monetary deprivation is punishment enough?'

'Of course, I do. In fact, even monetary deprivation could be avoided if women were given the right to bear children out of wedlock.'

'My question is, why are these strange rules against the religion we practise even necessary?'

'Because the world is still a jungle. The unevolved souls who inhabit the jungle are busy starving those who serve the cause of human progress. Society is unwilling to support those whose work does not bear instant fruit. The work that people engaged in research do will bear fruit in the future. Without social support, they must give up on marriage if they plan to continue with work which brings them no earnings. They are forced into celibacy unless they find women who will support them. I was fortunate to find such a woman. More than half the credit for the work I have managed to do in my lifetime goes to my wife. She cared for me, earned money for both of us, left me free to do my work. She was educated. That is why she understood and admired my work. She got her reward at dinner time when I shared with her what I had been reading during the day. When I undertook a major research project, she would discuss it with me. She was more than a wife. She was a partner in my research. With a wife like that I felt I was richer than any wealthy man I knew. She did not let me feel the pinch even when I needed to travel. She would borrow money on the strength of her salary, which was one hundred rupees a month. She would return the loan the following month by running the house even more thriftily than usual.'

'With a wife on whom you depended for everything, how can you still go around saying women should be free to leave their husbands whenever they wish?'

'Do you find that paradoxical?'

'I do indeed.'

'But it isn't. My wife did have full freedom to leave me if she wanted to. But she did not. She stayed of her own free will. Perhaps having full freedom, she did not feel the need to use it.'

'Such rules work with women who are learned like Shardabai was. It doesn't work with ordinary women.'

Vaijanath Shastri looked pleased with what Appasaheb had said and turned the conversation around to his wife, her life and her wonderful qualities. Later, he told Appasaheb that once he had thought through and worked out his ideas in detail, examined them for internal contradictions and illogicalities, he would be ready to speak of them with greater assurance. On their way back home, he said that could happen as soon as their next meeting.

Appasaheb decided that even this meeting with Vaijanath Shastri had not been as disappointing as he had thought at first. He saw a great similarity between Vaijanath and himself. Both had ideas for a future society that would be a step forward from where they were. And both were waiting patiently to see how far they could take them, in the present.

24. Kalindi's Decision

The discussion Kalindi had had with Ramrao before coming to Pune had one significant effect on her. She came to understand her own feelings on a vital subject. That night she had lain in bed thinking. Chintamani was not with her; yet he was before her every moment of the time. Her thoughts were as much about him as about herself and Ramrao. She realized that Ramrao was a man devoted totally to a social cause and least concerned about personal happiness; and she herself wished very much to be able to spend her life with him. However, the intensity of this desire was matched or perhaps even exceeded by a wish to not ruin his life. She mentally compared Ramrao's future with her to her father's life and wondered if it would be as painful. She had blamed her father for having married her mother, indeed often taunted him about it. Would her children do the same to Ramrao? The thought led her to the uncomfortable admission that she had not been fair to her father. She also knew that the consequences of her marrying Ramrao would be worse for him than the circumstances into which her mother's marriage to her father had thrown him. Her mother's conduct before marriage had not given society cause to be critical of her; whilst she had become infamous as the girl who had brought a bad name to the class of well-educated women. Ramrao would surely come to regret his action deeply if he did decide to marry her. Even conceding that he might be generous hearted enough to forgive her for her past life, he would still have her family's past to contend with.

The question she asked herself was whether the wise thing to do would be to follow the advice that Manjula Ajji had given her mother. She had said that lies did not work in marriage. It never ended with one lie. It became a series of lies causing constant friction between husband and wife. The children would surely notice this and begin to wonder what the problem was. Sooner or later, they would have to know about their mother's past. That would be a greater shame than making an honest confession to Ramrao at the start and get it over with.

Kalindi felt being honest should have nothing to do with hiding things from the children. They would grow up and discover her past anyway. So why allow that fear to scare her away from marrying Ramrao? He did not care a whit about who belonged to what caste. Her father had suffered because he had not expected to face the consequences he did from his caste. Had he chosen to marry her mother in the full knowledge of what would follow, he would have suffered less. Since she did not want Ramrao to suffer the same way on her account, the thing to do would be to warn him of all the consequences that would follow his marrying her. If he was willing to face them, there was nothing to hold her back from tying the knot with him. A man who looked at the road ahead with clear eyes before stepping on to it, one who was himself a brahmin and was therefore considered beyond blame by society, was the perfect man to champion the cause of people such as her and her children—bastards and outcasts. Her father had wished to rebel against society's rules but had not taken the next step to actually start a revolution. Ramrao, on the other hand, was already directly involved in starting a revolution. If he was prepared to marry her, it would be foolish to reject him for the imaginary hurts it might cause him. Kalindi was now certain of what she must do.

25. Ramrao's Ideas

Ramrao was not content with being a labour leader. He wanted to change the very system on which the textile industry in Mumbai was run. To that end, he had been reading up on the American experience of running mills and comparing them with the methods that Indian mill-owners were using to run their business. The time he had spent working as a clerk with Murar Deepchand had given him a lot of very useful information in this regard. His ideas had sprung from that experience and he was keen to share them with his fellow union leaders and with Kalindi. Their response would help him refine them further. It is not possible here to go into the minute details that were ultimately incorporated in the paper he wrote on the subject. What we can do is to present a condensed version of what the paper contained.

Ramrao's main argument was that workers in India were paid much less than anywhere else in the world and the reason for it was twofold—the owners' greed fed by the ease with which they could exploit the worker. The solution to the problem was to find ways to bring pressure to bear on owners to treat workers as co-workers and divide profits equitably between themselves, the management staff and workers or for workers to take over the mills and run them on cooperative principles. Why could mill-owners in Mumbai not do what even Americans were doing with such ease? They not only paid their workers higher wages but also sold their products at a cheaper rate. So why could this not be done in Mumbai? And why did mills have to be shut down so often? The owners' answer was to blame the workers. But Ramrao's answer was different. He maintained that managers as a class were idiots and deserved to be thrashed. Not that they were not clever. Of course they were. But all their wit was channelled into thinking up tricks to cheat, from the time land was bought to set up a mill. They knew how to double the actual price paid for the land on the sale deed. They knew how to over-invoice the cost of the machinery. Once the mill became operational, they found ways to turn the hands of the clock back to get a few minutes' more free work out of the workers. It was for such clever tricks that owners saw themselves as pragmatic and efficient.

During a conversation he had overheard between Murar Deepchand and Gokul Lalchand about old times, he discovered that the capital used to set up mills was actually half of what was shown on the books. He had naively thought then that mill-owners should not cheat in this fashion. They should think of themselves as workers who happened to be in a position to employ other workers. They should not look upon their employees as obligated to them or as easy prey. They should see them as fellow workers. If they stopped being greedy and were willing to pay their workers well, the workers in turn would be happy with their lot and work with a will. Owners would not need to hire musclemen and add to their expenses by having to submit to their demands for the gang's body-building costs. Should the welfare of employees not be the owners' prime concern? Should selling their products at a price to suit the pocket of the general public not be their aim? If they were not fulfilling these fundamental requirements that defined who they were, didn't they need to be thrashed? Leaders of the freedom struggle had called on people to wear home-manufactured cloth. Mill-owners, in full support of the call, instantly raised the prices of their goods. Why would the Congress Party have any objections to this? The ones to protest should be mill-workers. And the only way to do this would be to take over the mills and run them as cooperatives.

This brings us to the scheme that Ramrao was currently working on and desired to share with Kalindi to gauge her reaction. The basic idea behind the scheme was this: Owners, as he had discovered during his time with Murar Deepchand, run their business from beginning to end on credit. They buy cotton on credit. When it is woven into cloth, the cloth goes straight to the moneylender's godown as security for a loan to buy the next lot of cotton. The owners do not invest a single paisa of their own money. On whose strength are they able to get credit? On the strength of the labour that workers put in, to turn cotton into cloth. If that is the strength on which they get credit, why should workers themselves not be able to get similar credit? Ramrao argued that when workers go on long strikes, they make do somehow on the pittance that the unions give them. Being on strike means doing no work at all. Now, if they were to work hard at full capacity for a fortnight without drawing salaries, they would immediately find themselves creditworthy.

Ramrao had worked out that a strike would be the best time for the takeover. Workers are on strike. The mill cannot operate without them. Workers devote their time to studying every aspect of running a mill. They equip themselves with new skills while they wait for mill-owners to give up. Finally, the mill closes down. The workers walk in and take over. They work hard. They sacrifice the fruits of their labour till the mill is up and running and so, finally, become the mill's co-owners. Ramrao's scheme dealt with the social aspects of workers' lives too which would have to be attended to when mills were taken over and running. One of the biggest problems in a worker's life was his occasional need to borrow money. Moneylenders were either Marwadis or Pathans. Their practice was to lend ten rupees, get the worker to sign for twenty or even fifty rupees and charge interest at the rate of two annas per rupee. In Ramrao's scheme, these men would be allowed to set up shop in workers' neighbourhoods only on condition that they adopted fair business practices and allowed their books to be audited by workers' accountants. He also proposed buying a plot of land outside the city jointly owned by workers, where they would take turns according to a roster, at tending vegetables while simultaneously benefitting by the fresh, healthy air they would breathe.

Ramrao was now busy working out the nitty-gritty

of his scheme, inviting local union leaders and workers to discussions, taking their feedback to refine it and even sending out cyclostyled drafts to his fellow union leaders who were currently enjoying the king's hospitality in Meerut jail. Several people told him he was building castles in the air while still applauding the principles behind the scheme. His colleagues from Meerut suggested that he should run pilot projects to test the feasibility of the scheme. That would also help him understand what modifications were required to make it feasible. What remained now was to read out the draft to Kalindi for her response.

She listened very carefully when he did. Her first remark was, 'My focus has always been on household expenses. I feel workers should not be paid the entire salary owing to them whether on a weekly or a monthly basis. The reason is that they are expected to pay rent at the end of the month by which time they have spent their salaries. If enough of their earnings were held back till the end of the month, they would not have to borrow money to pay rent which they do all the time with the present system.'

'That's a good point. I must include it in the scheme.'

Next Kalindi said, 'Cloth must be made affordable for the poor. I wonder if a part of workers' labour could be paid for in kind, with cloth. Our workers are very poorly dressed, which is not good for their self-esteem.' Ramrao said he would give serious thought to the idea.

Kalindi's next remark was not a response to the scheme at all. She said, 'I am surprised that you show such concern for workers' welfare when you are not a worker yourself, whilst workers themselves seem not to care too much about themselves.'

'Why does that surprise you? I may not be a worker now, but I could say I was one not too long ago. I worked to advance my boss's interests then, and did not think up schemes to advance mine. I got disgusted with my work when I realized I was helping my boss to exploit workers. I read a lot in those days and discovered that the American industrialist had arrived at a less exploitative relationship between himself and his employee. There was a greater sense of their being fellow workers which guaranteed a slightly fairer deal for workers than we see here. It is possible for them to do this because they have developed efficient practices. Our mill-owners feel no responsibility either towards workers' welfare or the interests of the buyer. That's why they don't see the necessity of constantly evolving efficient management practices. Our managers are not invested in improving business methods because their methods fetch them more than they deserve. Once workers become owners, they would automatically make every effort to improve business practices because they would be the direct beneficiaries of all such improvements. My idea is to educate workers to bring about this revolution.'

'How do you plan to make your ideas available to workers?'

'I want to start a newspaper called „ The Real Revolution„.'

'Oh dear,' Kalindi said with a twinkle in her eye. 'That means you'll have to get yourself a new visiting card. It will be a little cluttered since it will say you are a lawyer, an editor *and* a workers' leader. But that can't be helped.'

26. Mill-owners Are Upset

Ramrao's scheme of turning mill-workers into mill-owners had been circulated so widely among the labour force that, inevitably, it reached the hands of some members of the Mill Owners' Federation. Ramrao was known to them for two reasons. The minor one was his having been a tutor to a member's children. The major one was the ruckus he had caused among them when he propagated certain views amongst the workers, which some of them had found dangerous. The Federation members had, for long, had Ramrao in their sights as a troublemaker. They had watched with interest the growing friction between him and other well-established union leaders, most of whom held that they had to fight on two fronts, against the imperialists and the capitalists, both being essentially allies. While this view had become received wisdom, Ramrao entered with a contrary view. He contended that the imperialists and capitalists were two separate entities to be fought separately with different weapons. The workers' present fight was against capitalists alone. When this news reached the Federation, a debate followed about whether his declaration was in their interest or against it.

Sir Sorabjee Chothia began by saying Ramrao sounded like a sensible fellow. Samuel Solomon who was deeply upset because he had heard that while Ramrao spoke against both Parsi and Jewish mill-owners, he had particularly disrespectful things to say about the latter. He therefore announced that Ramrao was a terrible fellow. 'We must protect ourselves against him for he is our true enemy,' he said.

Sir Sorabjee disagreed. 'Look,' he said. 'If our workers believed that the government are not at all our allies, their attitude towards us would soften. To be allied to the government would compound our original sin with another that could be termed traitorous. Once this idea gets out and about among the public, we would win their sympathy which would only help our cause.

Samuel Solomon, adhering to his own argument, said, 'How can that help our cause? On the contrary it would harm our cause irreparably if people did not believe the government is our friend. Many take us to be government officers. That helps us keep workers under control. If we want a disciplined work force, workers must fear us. If they believe that we carry the government in our pockets, they will be afraid. I would want this belief to grow in strength because then, workers will not take their grievances to the government even if we whip them. If people must promote their theory about our being on the wrong side of the government, let them do so in the English press. There we will benefit by the educated reader's sympathy. But if the workers begin to believe that the government is opposed to Indian industry and that, in a fight between us and them, the government will be a fair judge, the workers will grow arrogant. What Ramrao is doing by contending that we and the government are far from friends, is exposing our weakness. He says making enemies of both imperialists and capitalists in a single struggle will reduce workers' strength, whereas fighting the immediate enemy will help them concentrate their strength. We must protect ourselves against such a man.'

Members who belonged to the Congress party now intervened in the discussion. They said, 'We must find a way to befriend Ramrao. At a time when we were trying to bring the workforce into our fold, showing them how we were working in their interests, Ramrao was persuading them otherwise, insisting that workers' interests would always remain independent of any political party's interests.'

'So what is to be done with this man?' members wondered.

Sir Sorabji said, 'Nothing for the moment.' Other members agreed with him and the debate ended there. And now Ramrao had come up with this radical scheme.

Samuel Solomon said, 'This man is a troublemaker. We must find a way to have him jailed. When he's out of the way, his scheme will remain on paper.'

Once again there was disagreement. Sir Sorabjee said, 'We should co-opt a brainy fellow like Ramrao.'

Solomon said, 'You think he'll let you? You said he's brainy.'

Sir Sorabjee turned to the other members of the Federation. 'What do you think? Suppose we found a way to get Ramrao interested in his own welfare rather than the workers', would that not solve our problem?'

'Now there's a bright idea,' said a member from the Bhatia community. 'If we can get his brains to work for us, we couldn't ask for more.'

'Some of the ideas Ramrao has noted in his scheme aren't bad at all. We could try them out ourselves. Selling our cloth cheap to the workers themselves for instance. And getting workers to rely on unions instead of Pathans for loans. We could actually pay the unions to equip them as moneylenders. That will benefit us further because the unions too will be beholden to us.'

The members thought Sir Sorabjee's plan was brilliant. The very next day Ramrao received a letter appointing him Assistant Secretary to the Federation on a monthly salary of five hundred rupees.

27. Aaba Meets Esther

Esther had just got dressed to step out when the postman handed her a letter. It was from Kalindi. The envelope felt slightly heavier than normal and Esther was tempted to read the letter immediately. Her errand was not so important that it could not be postponed to the following day. She settled down to read the letter.

The letter began with Kalindi thanking her for introducing her to Sarah Ashtamkar and her daughters. It had been almost a year since she had been staying with them and she had gotten as comfortable there as she had been in Esther's home. That had been her first introduction to the Bene Israels, their ways and their problems. Her stay with the Ashtamkars had extended that knowledge. She had been enormously surprised by some aspects of their life that had been revealed to her. She was interested to find several bonds that connected them with Marathi people. First of all, she was amused to hear the Marathi words they had devised for festivals like the Passover. It was a surprise to discover this parallel universe of Marathi words she had not known existed. She was equally excited to discover that they used the kirtan form of storytelling and singing to propagate their religion. And finally, she discovered that the community was as fond of theatre as Marathi people were. They had plays of their own, written in the popular music theatre form of the times. The play Mrs Sarah Ashtamkar praised most highly was called *Queen Esther, The Musical*.

Esther found herself smiling at the excitement of discovery that brimmed over in Kalindi's letter. Perhaps she was still wearing the smile when the doorbell rang. She opened the door. On the doorstep stood a young man who looked vaguely familiar. The young man found the smiling woman before him just as familiar. Recognition dawned. She was the girl whose handkerchief he had picked up at the cricket match where he had gone with his friends. She had smiled when she thanked him. That was the very smile that now greeted him, accompanied by a warm invitation to come in and take a seat. As he sat down, he remembered how his friends had teased him about it for days afterwards. 'Have you proceeded further with the girl?' When they realized that he had not followed up on his chivalrous act, they had declared him an idiot of the first order. The memory brought an embarrassed smile to his face which dimpled his cheek. The dimple confirmed to Esther that this was indeed Aaba, more grown up, more of a man, but still the same.

An awkward silence had descended between the woman and the man, caused as much by memories of the past as the present circumstances that were about to create a new link between them. Aaba was the first to break the silence. 'I'm Kalindi's brother Satyavrat,' he said. She smiled. On the surface the smile was a polite acknowledgement of his self-introduction. But under it lay the secret thought, 'I know you better than you think.' Realizing that she was still holding Kalindi's open letter in her hand, she excused herself and went indoors. While there, she took a quick look at herself in the mirror and ran a comb through her hair to settle a couple of stray strands. She was rather pleased that Satyavrat had dropped in at a time when she was dressed to go out. When she returned to the sitting room, Satyavrat decided she was a very attractive woman. To cover up for this guilty thought, he adopted a brisk tone saying, 'First of all I must apologize for dropping in on you without notice. But I had to come to express my gratitude for the way you supported Kalindi when she was in trouble, despite the fact that you couldn't have approved totally of the circumstances that had brought on her difficulties.'

'Please, there is no need for gratitude. What I did was nothing. She was an old friend and we do these things for friends, don't we?'

'That may be so but my family should have acknowledged what you did when they heard about it from you.'

'I wasn't hurt or angry. Had they loved Kalindi, they would have thanked me for sure. But since they had broken off all relations with her because of the choices she had made in life, it followed that they would actually not take too kindly to me for the support I gave her.'

'It was not that at all. You did not meet my father. He would have done the right thing. You met my mother who somehow didn't have the presence of mind for it. But she hasn't stopped talking to us about you with gratitude.'

'There is really no need to feel grateful. I'm only happy to hear you don't hold what I did against me. And I'm happy you have come to say so.'

Aaba looked at Esther appreciatively and quickly changed the subject to the second reason for his visit.

'I've come for another reason too. News of Kalindi. How is she?'

'I've just received a letter from her. Besides talking excitedly about her discoveries regarding the Bene Israels, the community I belong to, she tells me once again that she is enjoying her work but is surprised that textile mills are not making expected profits despite the strong support they are receiving from the agitation for using home-produced cloth. She ends her letter as usual with regret. She misses her son very much.'

Just then Esther's mother came in with Chintamani.

'He looks so much like Kalindi,' Aaba said and stretched out his arms to the child. Chintu hopped into them quite readily. For a while then, the uncle played with the nephew and the nephew looked pleased with the things he was doing to entertain him.

'You'll make a good father,' Esther observed spontaneously.

'I don't know about that,' Aaba replied. 'But I will admit to being very fond of children.'

'Well, that's what being a good father means. Most men withdraw when children are born. They believe children are for women to bring up. They have no idea how important it is to a child's growth to have a father's presence and love.'

When finally Aaba handed Chintu back to his adopted grandmother, Esther said, 'I feel rather jealous of you.'

'Me? Why?'

'Because of the wide experience you have had of the world at such a young age. You have travelled all over the north and met such a variety of people. That has helped your mind grow and your thinking to mature.'

'Has my thinking matured? How would you know about that?'

'Kalindi has shown me the letter you wrote to her. I know how you have spent your time in the north. You have tried to persuade every person you've met to buy and read the Mahabharata. That can't have been an easy thing to do. I once sold tickets for a play that was going to be staged to raise funds for the welfare of the community. How difficult it was to make people part with their money even for a cause like that! I think you have done a great service to literature. The efforts of an ordinary man like you do more for books than one-time grants given by royalty.'

'I had no idea I was doing such useful work. Even my employers haven't said so,' Aaba said laughing. 'But tell me, when is Kalindi coming to Pune?'

'I don't think she's coming this weekend. But she is very keen that you should go to Mumbai to meet her.'

'I could do that if that is her wish.'

'If I am free, I too would like to see her there. I hope you won't mind if I accompanied you.'

'I'm sure Kalindi would love to see you.'

'But on second thoughts, I think Kalindi should come down here to meet you. You could come over when she is here. It would be a lovely get-together.'

Esther's mother came in then with tea and biscuits. The biscuits were locally made.

'You too buy local biscuits? How wonderful!'

'These are truly local. Made in Pune! We love them. So much tastier than the British ones we get.'

Satyavrat's opinion of Esther ascended a few more rungs.

28. Ramrao Decides

Kalindi was sitting with Ramrao in his office when a peon from the Mill Owners' Federation came with a letter for him. Kalindi felt a twinge of fear. Had the Federation got wind of Ramrao's latest activities and sent him a threatening message? But Ramrao laughed as he read the letter and she felt a surge of relief. The peon asked him if he should wait for a reply. Ramrao said tell your sahibs it will come to them by post. When the peon had saluted him and left, he handed the letter to Kalindi. She was extremely happy to read the contents. 'Congratulations!' she said. 'Why didn't you send your affirmative reply with the peon?'

'Because there's a chance my reply will not be in the affirmative.'

'Why ever not? Workers' welfare means everything to you and here's a chance for you to be in a position to bring it about. Why should you not accept the offer?'

'I am not at all sure that accepting the offer will help me improve the workers' lot.'

'Why should you not be sure? This job will give you more power to do that than being a union leader.'

'Wherever I am, whatever my job, I will make sure I can advance the welfare of workers. But what makes you think I will have more power to do that in the job than I have doing what I do?'

'In the course of my work, I have noticed that some mills are run more efficiently than others. Workers are better off there than they are in mismanaged mills. If the Federation can issue a manual of best practices to all its members, will we not have better-run mills and consequently happier workers? As assistant secretary you could make suggestions like these to benefit workers. Why do you hesitate to take an opportunity that has come knocking on your door?'

'Because I'm not as sure as you are that it is an opportunity at all. I need time to think. My gut tells me don't accept the offer. It is against my principles. But somewhere I find the offer tempting too. I must ask myself why, and for that I need time.'

A group of workers trooped in just then, looking agitated. 'The red flag is in retreat in the Parel neighbourhood. All the chawls there are now flying Congress flags. The Congresswalas came to our neighbourhood with their flags asking us to take down the red flag. We refused. There was a hot exchange between us. Then they said, fine, keep your red flags flying but fly the Congress flags as well.'

'So what did you say to that?' Ramrao asked.

'We said, will you fly the red flag alongside yours on your office? If you do then we too will fly your flag beside ours.'

'That was a clever answer.'

'We are not against them. If they ever require help, we'll offer it to them. But not at the cost of where we stand and who we think really cares about our welfare. The Congress is not dominated by workers but by owners. It is not our party but their party.'

While this conversation was going on, Kalindi's ears were pricked in that direction but her eyes were scanning the latest issue of *The Real Revolution*. Ramrao's editorial was about his scheme. He was trying to persuade workers to think seriously about it. It was not an easy task. The workers had many doubts and reservations. Kalindi read a letter to the editor written by a reader with great interest. 'Dear Sir,' it began. 'You talk about workers taking over mills. But how can this be done without a leader? We workers are illiterate. We do not have the skills required to borrow money from the market. Looking for even a fortnight's credit on cotton would be beyond us. Why do you not lead the way yourself? We will give you all the help that we can. Your humble partner, Ganpat Tukaram, clerk, Folding Department, Chandrika Mills.'

When the workers had left, Kalindi asked Ramrao once again, 'So? What have you decided?'

'Not to accept the offer.'

'Ramrao, I think you are making a big mistake. You are letting go of this opportunity that has come your way to run after some impossible dream.'

'There are reasons why I have decided to let go of what you see as an opportunity. One, I doubt very much if as assistant secretary I will have any powers at all to effect any changes in the present system and practices. Two, even if

I did have the power to do that, why should I share my ideas with owners who will only use them to increase their profits without passing on any of the increase to workers? My aim is not to empower mills by improving their management systems. It is to empower the worker. That is the chief reason why I have decided to turn down the offer. I have neither knowledge nor experience of the production side of textile mills. I know how to fight on behalf of workers and I must continue to do that. I must thank you for helping me come to this decision.'

'I? How can that be? I have been arguing in favour of your accepting the offer.'

'Precisely. To hear the opposite point of view and to argue against it has clarified my thoughts.'

'Please think again. Better business makes a stronger nation. It also puts us in a better position to compete with other nations.'

'I'm afraid my aim falls short of national and international goals. My aim is only to do everything I can towards more equal wealth distribution that will help workers get the fruits they deserve of their labour.'

'You don't think improving the running of mills—even keeping them alive which seems doubtful at present—will help workers?'

'Oh, I'm sure there are other, better brains than mine that are busy working on that aspect of things. I'm not required there.'

'Ramrao, may I ask you a question?'

'Please do.'

'Why do you hate mill-owners so much?'

'I don't hate them. As an aside, let me tell you the owners are not really the owners at all. Shareholders are the owners. But apart from that, I think it is downright immoral for some people to feast while others starve. If I can do something to create a more moral society, I would feel I have contributed to the betterment of the world.'

29. The Friends Make a Plan

When Kalindi arrived in Pune the following Saturday, Esther immediately sent a message to Satyavrat asking him to come and meet her. He sent a message back to say he would come the next day in the afternoon.

'So my brother turned out to be the same young man you had seen, didn't he?'

Esther smiled and nodded.

'Did you pinch his cheeks then?'

'I wanted to but had to resist the urge. Now that you're here, I'll do it in your presence.'

'Do you want me to tell him how you feel about him?'

'Certainly not. What you can do though is make sure he comes here often. Send things for him here which he will have to come and fetch or send things for me there which he will have to come here to deliver. Make it possible for us to meet as often as possible so our friendship grows.'

'That sounds like fun. Let me start planning for it.'

'Tell me, what does he like to eat? I'll make it for him the day he comes over.'

'Esther, you've thought up a complete strategy, haven't you?'

'My dear friend, I'm twenty-eight. Am I to ignore an opportunity that has come my way?'

'Certainly not. I think it's a wonderful opportunity for Aaba too. It's not going to be easy for him to find a girl willing to marry him. My family's history will affect him as much as it did me. He's a little younger than you. But that makes no difference to me.'

'You still haven't told me what he likes.'

'Everything spicy—chivda, chakli, kadboli...'

'Bhajis?'

'That too, but we don't make them at home. He eats them in teashops. We only make things that he can't get outside. But he loves bhajis. Once, before he was old enough to go to teashops on his own, Aai decided to make so many bhajis that even he would have to say enough. She made a huge heap of them. He ate them all. When she asked him if he had had enough, he said my stomach has had enough but my palate wants more.'

'That's decided then. I shall make them. Or if he prefers teashop bhajis, I can send for them. You get piles for just four annas.'

There was a pause in the conversation. Then Kalindi said, 'Would your community approve if you were to marry Aaba?'

'Of course it won't. It will say the girl has gone astray.'

'So then?'

'So then nothing. Look, I would have to bother about what they say only if I married within the community. If I marry outside, how would their approval or disapproval affect me? All I would want is for my family to accept the marriage. They won't initially. But I'm sure I'll be able to bring them around.'

'How will you do that?'

'I'll say if a Bene Israel man marries outside the community his act will pollute the family because he'll be bringing an outsider in. But that won't happen if a Bene Israel girl marries outside the community because girls belong to their husbands' families. Their families might object if they have rules like ours. But our family will remain pure.'

'That's all very well. But doesn't your community count heads? Won't they be upset that the community has lost one member and potentially more because that person's children too are lost?'

'Who can say anything about what might or might not happen? Years ago, a brahmin man married a Bene Israel girl. There was a huge to-do about it in the community. But their daughter married a Bene Israel man. One went out, one came back. Quits.'

'It won't be so easy in your case. Your community will hate losing an attractive, gifted, witty young woman like you.'

'I'll make them a promise. I'll send two of my daughters back into the community to make up for the loss!'

The friends laughed. Kalindi said, 'Look at us. Planning your daughters' marriages when your own is still undecided.'

'Castles in the air. Costs nothing to build them. In the end, if I don't get my prince and his castle, at least I'll have built one in the air for myself!'

30. A Young Man Pursues Usha

It was 6:15 in the evening. Usha and Satyavrat were at West End cinema to see the talkies. As they entered the auditorium, a young man tipped his hat to them in greeting. Satyavrat nodded in acknowledgement. He did not notice at the time that Usha had averted her eyes, ignoring the young man totally. He had nodded his head instinctively in response to the young man's gesture, wondering later if the young man was known to him or to Usha. As soon as they took their seats he said, 'I haven't been able to place the young man who just tipped his hat to us. I suppose I have met him somewhere, but I don't seem to recall exactly where.'

'I'll tell you about him later,' Usha replied.

'You mean you know him? So his greeting was to you then.'

'I don't know him nor do I want to. But it seems he wants to force his acquaintance on me.'

'But who is he?'

'I have no idea. He was here once before when I had come with a friend to see the talkies. That was the first time he tried to speak to me.'

'What did he say?'

'He asked me if I was a fan of Maurice Chevalier's singing.'

'And what did you say?'

'I thought he was addressing my friend. He was well-dressed. He could easily have been known to her. So I looked at her waiting for her to reply. But she was looking at me expecting me to reply. In the end neither of us answered him.'

'That must have embarrassed him.'

'Not in the least. He was standing outside when we came out. He offered to get us a tonga. My friend told him not to bother. He bowed and went away. We were at Empire cinema a few days later and there he was again. He bought a ticket after us so his seat was right next to mine. When there was a kissing scene in the film, he muttered, „ Lucky fellow.„ And when the couple hugged, he said, „ Go for it boy.„ I also suspected that he was peering through the dark to make out our expressions when he made these comments. He left during the intermission and returned with chocolates. He insisted we have some. We refused. He pressed us further. We still refused. He looked crestfallen. Finally he recited a Marathi couplet: „ If a worm, persevering, entered a rock / I too will one day enter your cruel heart.„ I realized then that he spoke Marathi. He had always spoken to us in English so I had taken him for a Goan.'

'Did you meet him again?'

'Today.'

Satyavrat and Usha emerged from the auditorium

during the intermission, he vowing to speak his mind to the young man if he showed up. They went to the restaurant. Usha sat at a table while Satyavrat went to the gentlemen's washroom. Sure enough the young man turned up saying good evening to her. Usha ignored him.

'Are you upset with me?' he asked.

She continued to ignore him.

'Tell me, what will you have to drink? Hot? Cold? Boy,' he called out.

Usha said coldly, 'I want nothing. Now please go away. If you don't, I'll call the manager and complain that you are molesting me. My brother is here. He'll be back soon. If you don't leave, there's bound to be trouble.'

'Why should I go away because your brother is here? I'll order something for all three of us. Why should there be trouble?' The young man was speaking calmly, quite unruffled. Usha said nothing while he stood draped over the back of the chair opposite. This is the scene Satyavrat saw when he returned. He felt an instant surge of anger but managed to control it. 'You see a young girl sitting alone and instantly take the chance to pounce on her,' he said to the young man. 'That is not gentlemanly behaviour, if I may say so.'

'True. But that's because I still haven't attained the status of a gentleman. I am only a college student. And I'm certainly not harassing this young woman. Just being polite.'

'Addressing a young woman with whom you are not acquainted is not the Indian way. Nor should a student behave in this fashion. Goodbye.'

'Why are you saying goodbye? Isn't it okay to talk to a woman once you are acquainted with her? You don't know people before you *know* them, right? When unknown people talk to each other they get to know each other.'

'But there are correct ways of getting to know a young woman.'

'If those ways were easy, everybody would have taken them. Had you been with your sister when I first saw her, I would have made your acquaintance first and hers through you. I'm sure you would not have minded introducing me to her then.'

'Don't be so sure of that.' Satyavrat's tone was sarcastic but his opposition to the young man had begun to thaw at the edges.

'Why should I not be sure? You look like a liberal man.'

Satyavrat had no answer to make to that observation. As a matter of fact, he rather admired the young man for his sharpness. Usha too felt amused by the young man's ready wit.

'You have no reason to assume I'm a liberal,' Satyavrat finally replied. 'And anyway, my sister is still a minor and I am not her guardian. Her father is. He alone has the authority to introduce you to her.'

'So what do you think I should do?'

'Not try to make a young girl's acquaintance in this surreptitious manner.'

'Surreptitious? I thought I was being very open. So according to you, if I feel attracted to a young girl, I do nothing about it?'

'Yes, unless you take the approved route. Approach

her family first for their permission. That is the courteous thing that society expects you to do.'

'Do you really believe that the attraction men and women feel for one another fits into what society considers proper? Would they allow them to be formally introduced to one another knowing the consequences? Our society disapproves of the very idea of men and women getting to know each other and seeing where their mutual attraction will lead them. That is why it has not created any conventions for this to happen in a natural way. So why not say we have become acquainted today and take the acquaintance forward towards friendship?'

'I don't grant that we are acquainted. I don't even know your name.'

'Benjamin.'

'So you're a Christian?'

'No. A Bene Israel. Korlekar.'

'And yet you have the gumption to try and make the acquaintance of a Hindu girl!'

'Mr Dagge, you don't know me, but I know you. I didn't expect you to hold that against me.'

'Why not?'

'Because I am distantly related to Esther Killekar. I happen to have seen you with her at the talkies last week.'

Usha turned to look at her brother. He looked discomfited but soon regained his composure.

'Yes, we did go to the talkies together. But I have not forced my acquaintance on her.'

'Because you have a sister through whom you got to know her. What should a man who doesn't have a sister do?' The intermission was over. It was time to go back in. On the way Benjamin Korlekar said to Satyavrat, 'I want your help. I have never crossed any line with your sister. I want your permission to talk to her if we meet again.' Satyavrat said nothing. However, at the end of the show, Bejamin Korlekar was at his side again. 'I wish to invite you and your sister to see the Saturday show of the next film. I urge you to accept my invitation. I should have introduced myself more fully earlier. I'm a student of the Grant Medical College in Mumbai. I've come down to Pune for my vacation.'

'I can't promise to come,' Satyavrat replied. But his voice was warmer than it had been.

On the way home Usha said, 'Benjamin has a point. Imagine him approaching our father to ask for permission to see me. Baba will want to know what his motive is. He will ask if Benjamin plans to marry me. But how can any young man intend to marry a girl whom he doesn't even know?'

'Yes, I can see how impossible it would be for a young man to ask a father's permission to see his daughter. The result would be nothing short of comical,' Satyvrat replied.

'Isn't that why you didn't let on to anybody at home that you took Esther out to see the talkies?'

'True. It would have led to all sorts of misunderstandings.'

'So what do we do now about Benjamin?' Usha asked. 'I must confess I wouldn't be displeased to talk to him if he approached me again. He seems to be a nice person.'

Satyavrat was caught in a bind. Instinctively he disapproved of his sister getting acquainted with a non-

Hindu boy. But how could he say so when she knew now that he was seeing Esther and had even taken her out to the talkies?

As the tonga turned into Sadashiv Peth, Usha said, 'So do we tell Appa and Aai about Benjamin and Esther today?'

'Of course not,' Satyavrat snapped. Then, in a more conciliatory tone he added, 'Nothing has happened that needs to be reported. For the moment, let this remain between you and me.'

31. Confession

Kalindi was climbing up the stairs to Ramrao's office when a young woman in a khadi sari passed her going down. Despite her simple sari there was something about the woman that suggested wealth. Kalindi wondered if she was the owner of the car she had seen parked downstairs. As the two passed one another, Kalindi thought the khadi-clad woman gave her a suspicious look. She was about to dislodge the thought from her mind when Ramrao's clerk came rushing out. 'Madam, you've left your handbag behind.' He held out an expensive-looking bag which the woman accepted with a thank you before proceeding downstairs.

'Who's that?' Kalindi asked the clerk.

'She's a mill-owner's daughter.'

Kalindi entered Ramrao's office with a wicked smile on her lips. 'No wonder you are turning down lucrative jobs,' she said as she sat down across the table from Ramrao. 'Which lawyer wants a mere job when he has car-owning clients lining up at the door.'

Ramrao laughed. 'Especially when car-owning clients come in the form of good-looking women.'

Kalindi felt the smile on her face freeze. Ramrao too noticed it and felt secretly gratified. Surely the frozen smile was a sign of jealousy and jealousy was a sign of the claim Kalindi believed she had over him? Gratifying though the thought was, it also made him uneasy. He was aware of his growing fondness for Kalindi. He was also aware of the social norms they had been contravening in seeing each other. While she was an independent woman who seemed not to care too much about what people thought or said, he had begun to feel guilty about exposing her to that kind of scrutiny when he had not even told her how he suspected he had begun to feel about her, leave alone proposing marriage which was the right thing to do. What had held him back from saying anything to her about his feelings was a certain episode in his past which she needed to know before he could broach the subject of marriage to her. The days when she came to the office, they talked about work first and then moved on to subjects that visitors who might drop in were welcome to overhear. When they went out for walks or occasionally to the talkies, they were too much in the public eye to permit private talk. It was also very difficult to begin a confession out of the blue with nothing leading up to it.

As it happened, Kalindi had come that day determined to continue the conversation about the job he had been offered and his decision to turn it down which they had left hanging in their previous meeting. Regaining her composure, she said with a laugh, 'Money makes even the ugliest women look good.'

'Would you say my client was ugly?'

'I'm sorry, but I didn't look closely enough to decide whether she was good-looking, plain or ugly. I was simply making a very general statement about the magical powers of money. Anyway, can we stop talking about trifles? I've come with a question. I want to know how you came to be so committed to the welfare of workers. Not just welfare either, but this radical idea of turning them into mill-owners. In short, your journey to this point.'

There was a long pause while Ramrao prepared himself to use her question as a starting point for his confession. Kalindi took the pause to mean Ramrao had never asked himself the question before and therefore did not have a ready answer. Deciding to prompt him, she said, 'The biographies of men and women who are driven by a single ideal always start with some incident in their childhood or adolescent years that triggered something that set them off on the path that became their life's work. Perhaps...'

Ramrao grabbed this opening to begin tiptoeing around his confession. 'You are absolutely right. It is indeed a personal experience that got me thinking and the process of thinking brought me to this path that I have chosen.'

'Am I going to be allowed to know what this experience was?'

'I have been meaning to tell you, but quite honestly I haven't known how or where to begin. I am tongue-tied even now. Let me try a roundabout route. Are you a reader of magazines?'

'Not an avid reader. But an occasional one.'

'Did you ever come across a story in a magazine called *Chandrika* written by a young man who had signed off as „ Unlucky or Lucky„.'

'As it happened, I did.'

'Would you believe me if I told you that the story wasn't fiction? That it was an account of something that had really happened to the writer and that the writer was me?'

'What are you saying? Did you really write that story? This is such an impossible co-incidence. I wrote the story to which your story was a response.'

'You are Nayadevabhagini? You could make story-writing your profession. It was such an engagingly written story. But whatever does that name mean?'

'Nayadeva is Yama. Yama's bhagini or sister is Kalindi. That's me.'

'What a macabre name to assume.'

'I was in desperate straits when I wrote it.'

'But your story had no details about actual events as mine did. It was a general account with a general question at the end, although you said it was a true story about a friend. She too had a strange name.'

'Upendravajra. That was also a made-up name. Her character and situation were both fiction in a sense, but in a sense not. They were based on the experiences of two or three college friends of mine whose stories I knew.'

'And their stories put you into such desperate straits that you called yourself Yama's sister?'

Kalindi looked at Ramrao a little nonplussed. After a long pause she said, 'No, that story had nothing to do with my state of mind. I shall tell you about that another time. But right now I am keen to know how being in love with a rich young girl and being rejected by her made you commit yourself to your present work.'

'I shall come to that by and by. But before I do, I must know how you felt towards the writer when you read the story. Did you feel, as many readers did, that the writer was merely boasting about his immoral behaviour?'

'Is that how people felt? No. I felt quite the opposite. I felt deep sympathy for the writer. Why did readers feel you were boasting?'

'Good question. Some even felt the story was fiction masquerading as truth.'

'Really? Why?'

'Because men are given to boasting about conquests they never made. Women are the exact opposite. Even when they are in fact having an affair, they will never admit to it. They do not enter relationships as conquering heroes.'

'Both lie but for different reasons. Both postures are false but they are what society forces upon them.'

'True. Society looks at them differently, doesn't it? Take a man and woman living together. The man will proudly declare she is his mistress. The woman will claim she is his lawfully wedded wife. The man wants society to know that he has the means to keep a mistress. The woman needs to show society that she has a legal claim to his means because she doesn't have means of her own.'

'Whatever society thinks, whatever readers said, you are now saying you were telling the truth. So let's return to my question. Why should being jilted, and the hurt it caused, become the trigger for you to choose this path?'

'Karunasundari wanted me as a lover but not as a husband. The only reason was my low economic status. Money became the deciding factor.'

'In marriage it always does, doesn't it? What's wrong with that?'

'I think it is morally wrong to live with a man with whom property is the only thing you share.'

'I can't be as harsh in my judgment of her as you. From what I remember of the story, she was already betrothed to the man she rejected you for. Financial transactions hinging on future marriage had already taken place. She too was caught in a trap, wasn't she? Even if she had wanted to, she couldn't have broken off her engagement because her father's ownership of his mill depended on the marriage going through. Would her parents have allowed her to turn her back on such huge benefits for the sake of love?'

'Perhaps you're right. But I still think there's a stink of immorality there.'

'Isn't it a well brought-up daughter's duty to obey her father?'

'There I disagree. I want to look carefully at the rules that govern family relations and throw out those that are founded on cunning interests.'

'Cunning interests? What could those be?'

'One is obedience to a father's wishes. Why should a father prevent his daughter or son from marrying the person they love and decide that they should marry the person he wants as son-in-law or daughter-in-law?'

'For their own good.'

'Not always. It is often for the father's good. Even royal families marry off their children for political ends.'

'If that is the case, then I would say both the daughter and the father were trapped by circumstances in your story.'

'But why had the father stepped into the trap in the first place is my question? Why did he contract his daughter's marriage without considering her wishes? Because he needed money. Why did he need money? Because money would ensure his continued ownership of his mill. Evidently, he had no other skills that qualified him to become its owner. A man owns a mill not on the basis of skills, hard work and efficiency, but on his ability to raise money from the market. This is the logical point to which my personal story had brought me. That triggered further inquiry. If I thought that ability to raise money was the only skill mill-owners possessed that allowed them to become so obscenely wealthy, then workers who brought labour and productivity to mills could be helped to acquire that skill. That would give them all the qualifications required to own and run mills.'

'I must grant your logic is impeccable. I understand your reasoning. But I have reservations about the thoughts you expressed earlier about marriage. You seem to think that love is all that matters in a marriage. That money should not come into the picture at all. But we know, don't we, that love alone has not been enough to keep a couple together?'

'Nor has money alone.'

'True.'

'I don't discount the importance of money. I was training to be a lawyer. I would have begun to earn well. But the point here wasn't enough money to live on. The point was to have more and more. It was greed. That is why I am so bent on working towards economic equality.

I do not believe it is good for the health of society for some people not to have enough to eat while others have so much that they become bloated.'

When Kalindi returned home that evening it was with a light heart. Ramrao had trusted her with a secret piece of his life which he would not have done had he not felt close to her. However, the next moment she felt guilty and downcast. She too had a secret, which she had not shared with Ramrao thus far. She felt his story could happen to any young man thrown together with an attractive young woman who even happened to share some of his interests. Her own case was totally different. Although circumstances had shown her that her future was a dead end and it was natural for a woman to try and find a path to some kind of future, it need not have necessarily been the path she chose. In a sense her case was also similar to Ramrao's. She too was thrown together with a man who seemed to care for her and also seemed to have the means to support her. It was inconceivable to her now why she had once felt the need to be supported. Having the same qualifications then as now, why did she not think she could find a job and support herself?

Her introspection brought her to a point where she decided she must, at all costs, look for any opening that her conversation with Ramrao offered to repose the same trust in him that he had in her. Kalindi went to bed with that honest thought in mind.

32. A New Sentiment Awakens

Ramrao was sitting in his office thinking of all the conversations he had had with Kalindi. The conversation in which she persuaded him that a woman who earned her own living was exactly the kind of woman that men like him should marry. The conversation about the job offer from the Mill Owners' Federation in which she had revealed that she cared more for money than he did. The most recent meeting in which she had shown a trace of jealousy about the woman who had visited him. Had she suspected that the woman was in fact Karunasundari? Over and beyond the indications he had received of how Kalindi felt towards him, there was also the ease he felt in her company. He had been greatly relieved that she had not judged him for his earlier involvement with a young woman. On the contrary she had felt sympathy for him. As for means, she had enough knowledge of the world to know that a lawyer does not remain poor for too long. Ramrao knew he had enough to go on for the moment and although he did not actively pursue money, he knew it would come sooner or later. Till then here was a woman who was financially independent and did not expect him to support her. Had he not argued with her in favour of a marriage that was built on love rather than wealth? If she considered him worthy of being her husband at this stage of his life, it would mean she too valued love over wealth.

Having come to this point in his thinking, he realized he did not need to resist the urge he felt when Kalindi stepped into his office. 'Kalindi,' he said gaily. 'Come, let's join our lives together.'

Kalindi sat down across from him in a state of happy shock. She was thrilled to hear those words from him, words that she realized she had been longing to hear for so many days. However, even as she allowed the joy to spread its glow through her body, she sensed another feeling welling up in the pit of her stomach; one of dread. The time had come to make her confession. This is the opening that she had been waiting for. She wished it had been a little more tentative, allowing her to beat around the bush before coming to the point. But it was so direct that it demanded an immediate and direct answer. Even then she stalled for time.

'You don't really mean that, do you?'

'I certainly do.'

'In that case I must tell you why you need to think a little more before you make the proposal. I am thrilled, I am grateful, but I am afraid you might not think me worthy of being your wife once you hear my story.'

'Why? Are you in love with someone else? Tell me who it is. I shall burn with jealousy but I will want to congratulate the thief on his luck. But Kalindi, I don't think the man, whoever he is, could love you as much as I do.'

'Ramrao, you are on the wrong path. You will not find the man you are looking for there. In fact, the man you are looking for doesn't exist.'

'What is the problem then? That you don't value my love enough to marry me? That's worse than the other thing. You are turning down my proposal because I don't measure up.'

'No, no. I am not turning down your proposal at all. I am just scared that, if I tell you what's keeping me from instantly saying yes to you, you will be the one to decide I don't measure up.'

'What is this great crime you have committed?'

'I don't know if I should tell you.'

'Of course you should. Get it off your chest.'

'First, you probably take me for a brahmin. I am not.'

'Have you ever heard me talk about caste? Have I ever tried to probe you about yours? Caste does not feature in my life.'

'True. But there's something else.' Kalindi paused to pluck up enough courage to speak out. 'Well...I must tell you...you should know...that I have been deceived in the past.'

'Is that all? I'm sorry to hear you have been deceived but frankly it makes no difference to my love. You should forget about it. Put it behind you.'

'I wish I could. But I can't. I have a son.'

'Where is he?'

'He lives with a friend of mine in Pune. That is why I go down every weekend if possible.'

'And the father? Where is he?'

'When I left him...or did he leave me...? He was in Pune. That was eight months ago. I haven't met him since.'

'Do you still care for him?'

'No, I don't. I don't want to ever set eyes on him.'

'Kalindi, let me first tell you that I do not respect you any the less for what has happened with you in the past. On the contrary, I feel even greater respect for you. But I will admit that, knowing what I know now, I cannot think of marrying you immediately. Let me explain. Let us suppose we marry. One fine day your son's father turns up wishing to see his son. I would have to let him in to our house, won't I?'

'Why should that happen in the first place since he doesn't care a whit about his son? And why should you let him see his son since he has not brought him up but I have?'

'Legally, you have his custody. The father has no claim over him. But I would not feel happy applying the law to the case. After all there is also morality. The man is your son's biological father and has every right to see him if he so wishes. So I would have to allow him to do so. But I'm not sure how I would feel about your old lover being in my house. I also cannot deny the fear I feel thinking that the bond which you once shared with this man might come to life again when you meet him and he shows concern towards your son.'

'That is impossible. I have not the slightest wish to have anything at all to do with that man again.'

'So you say now. But I have seen cases, admittedly in the working-class neighbourhood, where a woman never loses a certain feeling for the father of her children, however impossible he might be to live with. Rarely have I seen women leave their children's father to marry someone else for love. I need time to sort out my thoughts about that.'

'I honestly can't understand how such a far-fetched idea even came into your head. Workers belong to a different class than us. What they do doesn't apply to us. There has to be more to this idea of yours than your observation of workers' lives.'

'Perhaps there is. Perhaps I am thinking of a novel I once read which had an enormous impact on me. The novel is by the great French novelist Emile Zola. The original title is *L'Assommoir*. I read it in English translation, *The Dram Shop*.'

'And that was a story about a woman returning to the father of her children despite loving another man?'

'Yes. It is about a laundry maid who falls in love with a man who is something of a charmer and starts living with him. Or rather, he moves in with her. They have two sons. Later he goes off with another woman. The laundry maid then marries a roofer. One of the sons she has had with her first lover falls ill, the roofer allows the child's father to come to his house to see his son. A few days later he finds that his wife has re-established her relationship with her first lover.'

'But that's a novel, Ramrao. That's not how life is or needs to be.'

'It is written by one of the greatest realistic novelists in the world. It is based on a great deal of research that he did in the working-class areas of Paris.'

'Again, the working class. And now Paris. How can you think what is realistic there could be realistic here?'

'I don't know. I confess I'm confused. I just need time to sort out my feelings.'

'I understand. And I am both happy and sad at what you have been saying. Happy because you have not judged me as immoral for having lived with this man and borne his son. That doesn't bother you and that is a great relief. What bothers you is the existence of the son. If he didn't exist, I would have been worthy of your love.'

'Love doesn't come into it. I love you anyway. We are talking about marriage, which is another thing. And it is not the fact that you have a son that bothers me. It is the fact that his father is alive.'

Ramrao was shocked at what he had just said. But it was out and could not be taken back.

'So in conclusion, let me say, even liberals like you find it difficult to accept single mothers as wives.' Kalindi's heart grew heavy as she pronounced the words.

When Kalindi returned home that evening, she went straight to bed without exchanging a single word with Sarahbai. Lying in bed looking up at the ceiling, she said to herself, 'The most important discovery today is that Ramrao loves me. I know I love him very much. Given that, I must do everything in my power to clear his mind of the doubts he has expressed. Once that is done, marriage will follow automatically.'

33. Shivsharanappa Returns

The train from Pune reached its terminus in Mumbai. A young man, hardly able to stand, had been waiting for it to arrive. As soon as the compartments were swept and made ready for the return journey, he entered the third-class compartment and lay down on one of the long wooden seats. Later a much older man entered, looked around and, although the compartment was quite empty, chose to sit on the seat opposite the young man. He had recognized him as his old boss and his present state brought a smile to his lips. He was dead drunk.

'Come on, Appashet,' he began. 'You don't want us to believe that you are reduced to travelling third class simply because you have gambled away a thousand and five hundred rupees today? That is chicken feed for the likes of you.'

The young man said nothing in response, merely smiled. The older man continued, 'So did you meet your Kalindi while you were in Mumbai? Not that she needs to meet you now. She's earning for herself.'

The young man smiled again.

'That's what women need men for. Money. She was

yours while she needed it. Now that she doesn't, she has turned her back on you.'

The young man continued to smile. 'That's the difference between a wife and a mistress. The wife doesn't leave you. You are her name, her existence, her security. A mistress is a free woman. You thought Kalindi was with you because she loved you? That's nonsense. It's the money. I know. I've lived longer than you. I too have sowed my wild oats. But I came to my senses soon enough.'

The young man smiled yet again. His interlocutor had not even noticed that the young man was not responding to anything he said. He was one of those men who love the sound of their own voice and can hold forth alone for great lengths of time. Even when he did notice the other man's silence, he merely shrugged. Perhaps he still thinks of me as an employee, he thought. Or perhaps he just does not wish to talk to anybody. Perhaps he does not wish to be addressed by anybody. His general demeanour made that pretty clear. No skin off my nose he decided and moved to another seat.

The train arrived at Chinchpokli station, passed it and reached Currey Road. No new passenger had embarked and the older man could not resist the temptation of resuming his conversation with Appashet. He moved back to his old seat and said, 'You must be wondering what I was doing in Mumbai. I must confess that I was here to make arrangements to improve my finances. I will now be richer by a couple of hundred rupees a month. I have just paid to have the bungalow that you had mortgaged, released. But I plan to hold on to your old Marwadi tenant. I am shrewder at managing my finances than you have been. The bungalow is now mine. Rather than live in it, I will make it pay. The Marwadi pays me thirty-five rupees a month.'

The young man said nothing. Merely smiled.

The older man continued, 'I too gamble. But I don't fritter away my winnings. I build on them. That is why I have prospered.'

The train had reached Dadar. The man turned away to study the passengers who were boarding the train. When he turned around again, the young man had slipped to the floor. He looked closely at him and wondered if he had passed out. The new passengers cried, 'The man is ill,' and instantly called the guard. The guard called the police. They questioned the passengers about the man. Did anybody know him? The chatterbox not only said he did but proceeded to give the police information that they didn't necessarily need. 'He lives in Pune,' he said. 'His name is Shivsharan. He's a trader. He has lost a thousand and five hundred rupees today in gambling. I doubt if he has any relatives in Mumbai. But an old mistress of his lives here. Her name is Kalindi. She works in the Labour Office. You might let her know if you so wish. Because there is no way you can inform his wife Thayamma. She and his mother Rakhmai live in Pune. No, no. Sorry. The mother passed away a few days ago. Thayamma is the daughter of a wealthy trader from Bangalore.' He gave his own name as Mallikarjun Madki.

The police gathered together Shivsharan's effects and took him to hospital. The doctors smelled alcohol on his breath. But even the strongest smell of alcohol could not have hidden the other smell that they got a whiff of. Opium. They set to work instantly, pumping out the contents of his stomach. Shivsharanappa regained consciousness around four o'clock the next morning mumbling, 'Kalindi. Kalindi.' Then he noticed his clothes had been changed. He groped around asking, 'Where's the letter? My letter.'

The nurse on duty checked the pockets of his shirt and handed him the letter he was looking for. Although he grabbed it, it was clear that he was very weak.

The following morning Kalindi entered Ramrao's office having thought carefully over the options, or lack of them, that she had regarding her relationship with him. Going over the previous day's conversation, she conceded that, on the face of it, Ramrao had been very frank with her about the reasons why he could not marry her. She remembered he had used the words 'just yet', which meant that he had not rejected the idea of marriage per se. He had only asked for more time to think about the new situation she had presented him with. While that was true, she could not help but look at the problem from another angle. Could it not be equally true that he had pounced on the fact of her having a son and the son's father still being alive to shake off the responsibility of marriage? Perhaps he did not wish to marry. Examining her feelings in the context of that possibility, she realized that she was unwilling to give up a future with him simply because he did not wish to formalize it with a marriage certificate. Could she not suggest to him that they live together without marrying? As far as she was concerned, she had decided long ago that if marriage was not going to give her children a legal status, that if despite marriage they were going to be looked upon as bastards, then what meaning did marriage hold? It was nothing but a financial contract. Living with Ramrao could not be any worse than living with Shivsharanappa had been. Her family situation had already deprived her then of the possibility of a marriage made for love. Why should she expect that to change now just because more years had elapsed between then and now?

However, Ramrao might have very different thoughts about it. Might he not think living together was immoral? She turned the word immoral around in her mind and realized that it did not fit the Ramrao she had come to know. He did not care for the moral rules that society had made. He did not subscribe to traditional ideas which had their source in religious beliefs. He had his own morality based on a belief in social equality.

When Kalindi walked into Ramrao's office her mind was made up. Ramrao had a visitor with whom he was in deep discussion; but he gave her a quick, tender smile that lightened her spirits. 'You have a very determined look on your face this morning, Miss Kalindi Dagge,' he said. 'Please sit down while I try to get rid of this friend of mine who has been pestering me with some outlandish idea of his.'

'The only way you can get rid of me is by consenting to do what I am asking you to do.' The man spoke with the obsessive perseverance of an evangelist.

'But you still haven't answered my question,' Ramrao said.

'What question? You throw riddles at me and accuse me of not solving them.'

'May I know what these riddles are? Perhaps I can help solve them,' Kalindi intervened.

'Our friend has an idea,' Ramrao said. 'He and his associates are planning to celebrate tomorrow's Pithori amavasya as Mother's Day. He has come to ask me for help in spreading the word in the labour district.'

'So? Where is the problem?'

'I am not sure these people's respect for mothers is genuine. I have offered my help on one condition.'

'Which is?'

'That if they really want to honour motherhood, they must honour those mothers who make the greatest sacrifice for their children.'

'And who are these mothers?'

'Single mothers. I would like these people to honour a single mother for bringing up a child without help either from the father or from society. That alone will prove the genuineness of their claims about respecting motherhood.'

'And suppose we don't have the courage to do that despite truly respecting motherhood?' asked the visitor rather helplessly.

'Then you don't get my help.'

'Isn't that a little drastic?' Kalindi asked.

'Not at all. I really do have doubts about the true motives of people who pretend to believe women are goddesses. I am not saying our friend here is dishonest in his intentions. But neither do I believe he is honest. I need proof if I am to believe that. Working for women's rights has become a fashion today. There's a cult of people who launch movements on behalf of women. Their movement does not pinch their pockets but it brings them close to government officials and women.'

'Are you taking us to be those kind of people?'

'I am not totally sure that you are not. For me, the proof of any deep belief is one's readiness to sacrifice something for it. In this case you should be prepared to face public ridicule for your belief.'

'Ramrao,' Kalindi said, 'You are right but only partially. You have set a condition by which this group of people will convince you that their motives for this celebration they have planned are genuine. But they are not the only people involved here. The celebration you are proposing involves a single mother. Have you asked yourself if she would like to be publicly exposed as a single mother?'

'Thank you, Miss Dagge. That is very true,' said the visitor.

'We would have to give her courage to face the public. We can bring the issue to public notice through newspaper articles. That would prepare the ground, make the public more receptive to the idea. It will also arouse the government to acknowledge that single mothers who are left to fend alone for their children constitute a social problem. Perhaps the government could be persuaded to create a fund to help them. There are many possibilities that could be explored to bring dignity to single mothers.' Turning to the visitor, Ramrao said, 'Come to me the day you muster enough courage to go along with these ideas and I will happily work with you.'

The messenger of hope for women had no option but to see this as an ultimatum and give up hope of acquiring Ramrao's cooperation. He left Ramrao's office totally crestfallen.

Kalindi took the chance to bring the conversation back to her problem. 'You seem to be suddenly all for single mothers. Have you had a change of heart?'

'Kalindi,' Ramrao said, a little hurt. 'Why do you say things like that? You know I have always felt that way.'

'Oh, I didn't mean in a general way. I was thinking of your rejection of me.'

'You have decided to deliberately misunderstand what I was saying yesterday. But I guess you were hurt that I didn't immediately agree to marry you but asked for time. I think you will be fairer to me once your hurt is eased by what I am about to say.'

'What?'

'That I've had a whole night to tackle the barrier that was holding me back from doing what I want to do.'

'And what is that?'

'Marry you.'

Kalindi was not sure she should allow her heart to leap as it was already doing without her permission. Ramrao rose from his seat and came round to her. Looking down at her, he said, 'I have no idea why I was comparing us to some remote characters in a French novel. But I'm glad I was. It helped me tell you of my fear. At night the thought came to me, surely you were a mature woman who knew what you were doing and saying. Surely you would make sure that the kind of troublesome eventuality I had foreseen would not actually come to pass. Wouldn't you?'

'Of course I would. I have no wish to see my son's father again. What happened, happened. I've moved very far away from those days.'

There was a window behind Ramrao. As he turned, he noticed three men jump out of a car that had just parked in front of his office. He recognized one of them as a policeman in plain clothes. 'Now what do they want with me,' he wondered. Just then his assistant burst into the room saying, 'Some people wanted to know whether Kalindibai is here. I said she was. They said they wanted to meet her urgently.'

Kalindi was taken aback. 'The police?'

Ramrao said, 'Send them in.'

The policeman he had recognized rushed in. 'Sir, there's a man lying in King Edward's hospital very ill, probably dying. He wants to see Kalindibai.'

'Who is it?' she asked.

'Someone called Shivsharanappa. He's from Pune,' the policeman replied.

Kalindi turned to Ramrao. 'I'm not going.'

'Who is this Shivsharanappa?' Ramrao inquired.

'My son's father,' she answered.

Ramrao noticed the tears she was trying to fight. He took her hand in his and squeezed it. 'I think you should go,' he said. 'Would you like me to come with you? I'll wait outside.'

'Yes please,' Kalindi said as she got up shakily from her seat. They made their way downstairs, got into Ramrao's car and headed straight for K.E.M. hospital.

34. A Letter of Revelations

Kalindi entered King Edward Memorial hospital and was led to the ward where Shivsharanappa lay. When he saw her standing beside his bed, he mustered a weak smile. Handing her a letter, he muttered 'Kalindi' and breathed his last. Kalindi burst into tears. All the anger she had felt against this man had melted away. Before her lay a human being who had once been full of life, full of himself and now lay lifeless in a city that was alien to him, among people who were strangers. She was the only other human being who had meant anything to him. He had held on to his last breath till he saw her. She was deeply moved.

Back in Ramrao's office, Kalindi opened Shivsharanappa's letter and began to read:

> May I have Lord Shiva's blessings.
>
> I intend to end my life today if I lose at the gambling table. Whoever finds this letter is requested to hand it over to Miss Kalindi Dagge of the Labour Office. I ask the government to ratify it as my last will and testament.
>
> There are many people who have judged me as

immoral and reckless, holding me responsible for ruining the lives of two women. I hereby wish to furnish information about my life that will, I hope, exonerate me to some extent of these charges. I was married against my wishes as the result of a plot hatched by my family and the matchmaker. The plot was furthered by my clerk Mallikarjun Madki who was bribed to assist in it. My wife Thayamma was seventeen years old at the time of marriage but had still not begun to menstruate. Her family was fully aware of this and the news had leaked out in the community. My uncle who was responsible for bringing about the marriage was certainly in the know. My father was dead and my uncle was now head of the family. My mother had no idea about the state of affairs, nor could she have opposed my uncle in the matter. The truth is, she saw a girl who looked well grown and assumed she was biologically mature too. Her family was rich and had promised my family a handsome dowry. That was enough for them to ruin my life.

I was in this situation, unable to see even a ray of hope in my dark future, when Kalindi came into my life. It was natural for me to fall in love with her. She too wished to show society that if they rejected her claim to legitimacy, she would do something to actually deserve their censure. To my great joy, she agreed to live with me. The moment of greatest joy for me was the birth of my son, my marriage having been barren. It was my love for her that drove me to neglect my business, allowing my evil clerk to take advantage of my long absences from the shop and build his own future on my ruin.

Those were dark days when I often thought of killing myself. What kept me from taking that step was the thought of how it would affect Kalindi's life. People would have surely held her responsible for my financial ruin and my consequent death. I felt, however, that the time had come to distance her from me. I wanted her to leave me, to make another life for herself since I was now unable to offer her and our son the security they deserved. The only way I could achieve this end was by behaving in a way that would tell her that I had stopped caring for her, that she no longer meant anything to me.

If this letter does reach Kalindi, I would say just this to her: not a single day passed after she abandoned me when I did not think of her and Chintamani. I hated myself for having destroyed her life. I was therefore overjoyed to hear that she had found a good job in Mumbai and was finally free of financial cares. My other source of joy was knowing that she had found another man who seemed to care for her. I must admit that I had seen the two together although I had taken good care not to be seen by them.

Chintamani has always been in my thoughts. I don't care that he is illegitimate in the eyes of the law. To me he is my son and heir. I was always careful not to put his inheritance at risk while gambling away mine. Before my mother died, I had got her to sign the house she had inherited from her mother in Hubli in Chintamani's name. She has also left for Chintamani the four thousand rupees which she has loaned to Govind Kadadi for his shop at twelve annas interest. Kalindi should now claim the house and the money for Chintamani's future. If she marries again (although we were not man and wife, I always thought of us as being married) her husband will not have to bear the responsibility of providing for Chintamani. I would like Chintamani to adopt the Shaivite religion. But I cannot order him to do it.

That part of Thayamma's dowry, which was meant for her, is safe. I have never touched it. So she too is taken care of. Although she was forced on me, although her family deceived me and destroyed my life, I never ill-treated her. When my mother realized how things stood between Thayamma and me, she tried to persuade me to marry again. I did not want to do it immediately. I waited to see if Thayamma would start menstruating. When people saw that I was hesitating to marry a second time, they spread the rumour that I did not have children because there was something wrong with me. The person who spread the rumour was again my sworn enemy, Mallikarjun Madki. When people asked him why I did not have children, he would say, 'If there's no water in the well, where will water come from in the water wheel?' Perhaps he meant to say the dry well was Thayamma. But people took it to mean me. So even if I had come around to the idea of marrying again, who would have given their daughter to me?

I have handed over my shop along with its goodwill to a customer who will take care of my debts. I am thus free of debt. I have with me two-and-a-half thousand rupees. I am setting aside five hundred for my funeral and burial. I request Kalindi to look after that. I am going to gamble with the remaining two thousand. If

> I win, I will live to see a better day. If I lose, I will kill myself and end it once and for all. In a very real sense, therefore, my future is a gamble.

Shivsharanappa's letter left Kalindi benumbed both with shock and sorrow. She handed the letter over to Ramrao without a word. He glanced through it and said, 'We have work to do.' He called up a couple of his Lingayat shopkeeper friends. They took care of the funeral arrangements and Shivsharanappa was buried with the rituals of the religion he had fervently believed in.

35. Changing the World

For a long time now Appasaheb Dagge had been introspecting. He had already admitted to himself that he had been wrong in his treatment of his children. He absolved himself of guilt to some extent with the knowledge that he had been severely tried. He had not foreseen how his marriage to a low-caste woman with a none-too respectable family history would impact their lives. When he saw how his well-intentioned act had ruined his children's chances of living as self-respecting human beings, he went into a shock that took away his powers of rational thought. It was in that state of mind that he had turned his back on Kalindi and later, on Satyavrat. Fortunately, his son was back with him and his daughter would soon return. Of that he was certain.

Appasaheb's introspection had led him to other realizations. He knew now that, what he had set out to do was too vast a task for a single individual like him to carry out with even minimal success. What was he after all? A barrister. What knowledge did he have of the Vedas, the Upanishads and the Smritis, which had given Hindu society its beliefs, laws and customs? Without that foundation, his ideas were like seed planted in surface soil, ready to fly away with the first gust of wind. He knew now that he needed to be part of a larger movement led by a personage of knowledge and spiritual stature. As part of such a movement, he would have the power—if anybody did—to change the rules that ancient sages had made.

It had become generally known that Vaijanath Shastri had been delivering sermons around the country about his ideas for social change. When Appasaheb had heard of his return to Pune from his long wanderings, he had sought a meeting with him to discuss the questions that had been bothering him. As we know, he had met him on a Sunday afternoon. The ideas that Vaijanath Shastri had expounded on the occasion had left him feeling more than a little uncomfortable. The savant had said then that he was in the process of refining his ideas further and they should meet once that was done. Appasaheb had met him a second time. This time he had taken Satyavrat with him. Vaijanath Shastri had asked Satyavrat several questions regarding his reading and recent activities and had appeared impressed by what he heard. He had said imperiously then, 'When I am ready with the *Vaijanath Smriti*, this young man will be my amanuensis.'

Satyavrat had not accompanied Appasaheb when he visited Vaijanath Shastri next. In the course of that meeting the scholar had confessed that he had still not been able to give a final shape to his ideas but that he would talk about some that he was certain of. This time he had no objection to sitting under a roof to talk. He had begun by stating that he had found a name for the new caste he wished to create. 'I hereby declare that the new caste will be named Rishimandal. As its founder, I wish to state that the goal before this group of visionaries, people who practise the most rigorous ethics regarding the welfare of the human race, is not confined to this country alone, but will apply to all peoples across the entire world.'

Despite this grand announcement, he returned once more to rules governing marriage which he said were all to do with money and property. He went on to expound ideas that he had not touched upon in their previous meeting. 'Young people wish to marry for love. However, those in authority, like their parents, urge them to think of the material aspects of marriage. There is neither love nor spirituality in their thinking. It is profane to discount love and think only of practical matters. We will therefore give men and women full freedom to cohabit for love and women the right to bear children in the assurance that their reputations will not be besmirched by society.'

Appasaheb had not been able to keep quiet when he said this. 'I must say I do not agree with that.'

'With what?'

'With what you just said. My heart and mind rebel against every word you have uttered.'

Vaijanath Shastri had given him a contemptuous look. 'That is because you are not strong in mind or spirit. We need men who are not enslaved to the present with all its rules and customs that belong to an ancient age when neither science nor technology had made the progress they have made today. You are scared of popular opinion, forgetting that your critics too are mere men, whether they are teachers, journalists or some fuddy-duddies from your Prarthana Samaj. When such people start parroting their usual nonsense, you should give them a couple of kicks in the ass and ask them if their sentiments are their own independent thinking based on their individual experience. If they say they are, you should give them a couple of more kicks and say,„ You donkeys, you are not even capable of speaking the truth.„'

It was on Appasaheb's tongue now to tell Vaijanath Shastri he was talking a whole lot of drivel, but he could not pronounce those words at least partly because he remembered how short the scholar's temper was. And yet, on his way home, he had granted that, although the ideas he had heard that day were impossible to swallow in their totality, it could not be denied that there was some truth in them. It was for this reason that he had remained curious about *Vaijanath Smriti*, the scholar's promised collection of rights, laws and conduct for a new world order. Vaijanath Shastri had already nominated Satyavrat his amanuensis. So he now took Satyavrat with him for what was to be the final meeting between them, the one that would help him make up his mind about whether he had found the leader of the kind of movement he was looking to join.

Vaijanath Shastri was ready for them when they arrived. He made it clear to Satyavrat that he had the freedom to organize what he was about to dictate as paragraphs if he so wished. He was also free to number the paragraphs if he so wished. What he was not free to do, however, was change a single word of what was said. With this he launched into a discourse that Satyavrat wrote down in forty-two numbered paragraphs. The first ten paragraphs laid out the philosophical, historical and sociological ground on which his ideas were based. The next ten paragraphs expanded on his thoughts on women's rights, and the freedom to be given to men and women to choose which system of family life—patriarchy or matriarchy—they wished to adopt. The first system would put the onus of earning for the family on husbands. This would automatically lead to a division of labour between them and their wives as existed in middle-class families. The second, matriarchy, put the onus of supporting the family on wives, which would lead to their freedom from rules that governed patriarchy. From here the discourse moved on to the social status of courtesans and their progeny and the need for both to be granted respect as equal citizens.

Paragraph eighteen contained the most radical idea of the discourse. Here Vaijanath Shastri exhorted single women to launch a militant campaign in favour of matriarchy. The paragraph read, 'I hereby call upon all women who have been left on the shelf by society and all widows who have been spurned by society to come together and fight against patriarchy. I assure them that such a battle will not be against religion but in favour of a better religion. As part of your campaign, I call upon you to raise a fund for single mothers who, because of social stigma, have not been able to fulfil their potential.'

At the end of paragraph forty-two, Vaijanath Shastri declared that he needed time to think over a few more points that he had in mind. He asked Satyavrat to return in four days to take them down, completing the *Vaijanath Smriti* manuscript. He said he would need to go over the discourse once it was written to check for repetitions and internal contradictions. Once that was done, he intended to publish his Smriti and wait to see if it inspired people to become his followers. He then repeated something he had said earlier. His ideas were not confined to Hindustan but were intended to create a united world that was more equitable and just than the present one.

Satyavrat found it difficult to swallow this idea of world unity. In his opinion it was too big a leap to take and he put Vaijanath Shastri's Smriti in the realm of fantasy. However, he brought the partly written manuscript home to make a copy before returning the original to its author. However, before he could do that, Appasaheb heard that Vaijanath Shastri had got scent of some old documents in Konkan and had gone off there to look for them. He stayed hidden there for two months at the end of which came news of his sudden death.

Of what use now was the half-finished manuscript in Satyavrat's possession? Although the ideas that Vaijanath Shastri had already dictated were adequate to build a movement on, who would believe that the manuscript was indeed dictated by him? It was neither in his handwriting, nor had he signed it as its author. More importantly, Appasaheb and Satyavrat were not at all sure how far they themselves were willing to go in support of his ideas, some of which appeared more fantastical than idealistic. All they were certain of, through personal experience, was how destructive a force patriarchy was. This convinced them that a change was urgently required, perhaps in the direction Vaijanath Shastri had indicated. For the moment, however, that was how far their thinking on the subject went. How their present ideas affected their personal choices will be revealed in the following chapter, the last in this tale of a family's battle against prevailing social norms.

36. The Happy End

I am not sure that it can be pronounced as a general truth, but it was certainly true in the case of Appasaheb Dagge and his family that personal happiness took the sting out of social evil. For years the Dagges had talked passionately about the urgent need for social change. Suddenly now the urgency of the task had lost vigour. It would have been possible to apply for permission to search the one and only tin trunk in which the ascetic Vaijanath Shastri kept all his effects. It is possible that the trunk contained the scraps of paper on which he was accustomed to jot down his thoughts. It is also possible that most of the points in the manuscript in Satyavrat's possession would have found their rough beginnings in those jottings. Those scraps could have been held up as proof that the manuscript had been prepared at his behest and as dictated by him. He had a large band of followers in Maharashtra. They could have been gathered together to start the movement Vaijanath Shastri had so desired. The movement could have borne his name to give it credibility, but the engine behind it would have belonged to his followers for whom his ideas on religion and society were beacons lighting their way to a new society, a new world. However, this was not to be. The world would have to remain unchanged while the Dagges fulfilled their personal destinies.

Chastened by his earlier missteps, Appasaheb was only too happy to give Satyavrat his blessings to marry Esther Killekar. They were madly in love and were strong enough together to face the possible displeasure of some members of her community. Many of them, as it turned out, were genuinely angry with her. But there were some who treated her with sympathy. Among them was Benjamin Korlekar whose interest in Usha had flowered into something a little more serious. She too had ceased to think of him as an intrusive pest and had gradually given in to softer feelings. The world thought they had met during Esther's wedding and fallen in love. Little did they know that the road to their ultimately becoming man and wife had its beginning in the screenings of English films in Pune city's cinema houses.

Kalindi, who came to Pune with Ramrao and Chintamani to attend her dear brother's wedding to her dear friend Esther, had long ago given up ideas of changing the world. She had found the kind of happiness she had never dared to hope for after the consequences that her rebellious act had led to. She would always support Ramrao's ideas for a more equitable society in which mill-owners would not be able to exploit workers for obscene personal profits; and in so doing, she would in fact be helping to change the world. That, for her, was enough given her new found happiness.

Appasaheb and Shantabai were now assured of an old

age in which they would have the love, respect and support of their children and their children's spouses. In a very strange and unexpected way, the leap that Appasaheb had taken into the unknown by marrying Shantabai had led to unforeseen satisfaction. Had he not broken social rules by his action, he would not have had the depth of vision to allow his children to find their own equally unconventional paths to personal happiness. And so, Appasaheb could at last sit back with an easy conscience and more than a trace of self-congratulation.

Dr Shridhar Vyankatesh Ketkar (MA PhD) was a sociologist, historian and Marathi novelist. Born in 1884, in Raipur in present-day Chhattisgarh, Dr Ketkar studied at Wilson College in Mumbai. During his graduation, he left for the United States in 1906, and obtained a master's degree and a PhD from Cornell University in 1911. He returned to India after spending a year in London, where he met his future wife Edith Kohn.

Dr Ketkar is widely known as the chief editor of the first ever encyclopaedia in Marathi, which comprised selected writings of Indian and European scholars, *Maharashtriya Jnanakosha*. He also published several scholarly papers, founded and ran three magazines and wrote six novels, each with a strong sociological theme. *Brahmankanya* (1930) was the fifth.

Shanta Gokhale is a bilingual writer, translator and theatre critic. Both her Marathi novels, *Rita Welinkar* and *Tya Varshi*, have won Maharashtra State awards and been translated by her into English. Her most recent books are her memoir, *One Foot on the Ground*, and *Shivaji Park*. She has translated *Smritichitre: The Memoirs of a Spirited Wife* by Lakshmibai Tilak, for which she received the Sahitya Akademi Award for Translation, 2021, and the novel *Kautik on Embers* (*Dhag*) by Uddhav J. Shelke, besides several plays. She is the author of *Playwright at the Centre: Marathi Drama from 1843 to the Present*; and the editor of *The Scenes We Made: An Oral History of Experimental Theatre in Mumbai*, among others.

She has received the Sangeet Natak Akademi Award for overall contribution to the performing arts and lifetime achievement awards from Thespo, Ooty Literary Festival and Tata Literature Live!.